RIDE WEST FOR WAR

Also by Chad Merriman in Large Print:

The Avengers
Night Killer
Blood on the Sun
Hard Country
Snakehead

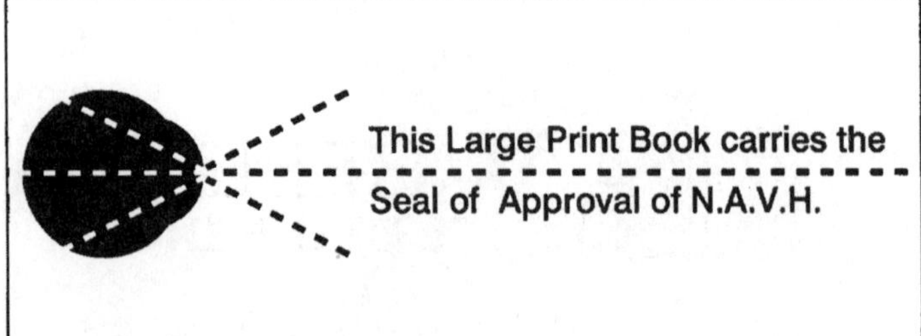

RIDE WEST FOR WAR

Chad Merriman

Published in 2005 by arrangement with
Golden West Literary Agency.

Wheeler Large Print Western.

The text of this Large Print edition is unabridged.
Other aspects of the book may vary from the original edition.

Set in 16 pt. Plantin by Minnie B. Raven.

Printed in the United States on permanent paper.

Library of Congress Cataloging-in-Publication Data

Merriman, Chad.
Ride west for war / by Chad Merriman.
p. cm. — (Wheeler Publishing large print westerns)
ISBN 1-59722-078-7 (lg. print : sc : alk. paper)
1. Large Print books. I. Title. II. Wheeler
large print western series.
PS3553.H38R53 2005
813′.54—dc22 2005016148

RIDE WEST
FOR WAR

National Association for Visually Handicapped
serving the partially seeing

As the Founder/CEO of NAVH, the only national health agency solely devoted to those who, although not totally blind, have an eye disease which could lead to serious visual impairment, I am pleased to recognize Thorndike Press★ as one of the leading publishers in the large print field.

Founded in 1954 in San Francisco to prepare large print textbooks for partially seeing children, NAVH became the pioneer and standard setting agency in the preparation of large type.

Today, those publishers who meet our standards carry the prestigious "Seal of Approval" indicating high quality large print. We are delighted that Thorndike Press is one of the publishers whose titles meet these standards. We are also pleased to recognize the significant contribution Thorndike Press is making in this important and growing field.

Lorraine H. Marchi, L.H.D.
Founder/CEO
NAVH

★ Thorndike Press encompasses the following imprints: Thorndike, Wheeler, Walker and Large Print Press.

Chapter 1

It was another desert river, this one the Carson, sliding slack and tawny under the sandy banks of its channel. The stage road had followed the dwindling stream from the sink where the stream disappeared. It had turned with the watercourse until now, Tracy Dalton thought gratefully, it pointed west again toward the regal Sierras that hovered over western Nevada. The 'dobe crackerbox of a change station stood in the bend of the river, crowded against it by a great valley of bald rock and dry brush. Hidden in the open distance to the south was Fort Churchill, bulwark of the fabulous Comstock silver region against the Indians of the desert.

The soldier who had picked up a mail pouch from the newly arrived stage had come from there. He was a corporal of the Fourth Cavalry, soon to leave for the seat of war in the East, and Tracy envied him. More immediately, he wondered if the noncom had spotted him. The grey dust rolling eternally with the Concord had wiped away his individuality, as it had that of the other passengers. His dress was the same as that worn by thousands of men ranging the mining camps of Colorado, Nevada and California. He was pretty sure the corporal had business with him, business that would have to be handled neatly.

This was a swing station, the type where the coach usually stopped only long enough for the teams to be changed, without the driver leaving his seat on top. But a wheel had complained for the last few miles, and this time the whipman had told his passengers to stretch their legs. Twenty-five miles more of late fall desert lay between them and Virginia City, the gaudy metropolis of the Far West, where most of the passengers were bound. So they had all got down, and all but one besides Tracy had disappeared. The one woman in the group, having tasted and rejected the brackish water in the barrel by the door, stood there now against the wall, impatient to be on her way.

She projected a total disinterest in her surroundings, but in the five hundred fifty miles from Salt Lake City Tracy had learned that she had much more feminine curiosity than she betrayed. All he had detected, besides, was that she was young, extremely pretty, wore a wedding band, and was a very determined young woman. For four nights she had refused to lay over at one of the home stations to sleep. Determined, he thought, or with some urgency on her to hurry. Or perhaps it was mere fastidiousness, for the bad food, worse beds and coarse company of the way stations were even less attractive than the swaying seats of the coaches.

The corporal had cinched the mail bag to his saddle but seemed in no hurry to start on the return ride to his post. He eyed Tracy briefly, then took a cigar from his shirt pocket and clamped it in his teeth. Convinced, Tracy walked over to the water barrel. The young woman moved away a step, and he drank. When he hung up the dipper, the corporal stood beside him.

Grinning, Tracy said, "They must have got that water out of a tanning vat."

"A man gets used to it. This your first time out?"

"First time west of Blackhawk."

The corporal was satisfied. "Got a match, sir? I seem to have come off without mine."

Tracy drew his matchcase from his pocket and extended it. The corporal turned slightly away from the girl while he lighted his smoke. When he handed back the case, Tracy saw that the switch had been made smoothly. He dropped the new container into his pocket and glanced at the girl. The stock tenders were hooking on fresh teams, and she was watching them idly. There was no indication that she knew code remarks, much less anything else, had been exchanged in her presence.

With a shout and a clatter, the stage ran on, the girl by the right window and across from Tracy, who rode backward. The road continued on the left bank of the Carson, which often vanished beyond a screen of astonishingly luxuriant sagebrush. The old man next to the girl dozed off, and the miner on his left sank into secret reverie. The men were all above military age, for the call for volunteers at the start of the rebellion had drawn off most of the able-bodied young men. Tracy knew that made him conspicuous for he was four years short of thirty, and certainly there was no impairment in his six feet of muscle-molded body. He wondered what the girl thought of his traveling ever west when pride, if not patriotism, should have taken him the other way. Well, that was a self-consciousness he would have to get over.

Yet he wished he could tell her how

bitter he had been when he had been turned back at Jefferson Barracks on a mission of whose importance he was not persuaded even yet. It might strike a spark of interest in that beautifully sculptured face in its frame of black hair. . . .

"No arguments, Lieutenant," the adjutant at Jefferson had said firmly. "Any tough young buck with an education can become a good field officer. Right now, that's not our problem. We have a crowding need, however, for a reliable man experienced in the West, particularly in the mining country. You are, and that's it. Report to Colonel Edgefield."

And this was all that had come from his rushing down the Smoky Hill from Blackhawk, Colorado, to get in the action in war-torn Missouri. His military academy background had got him a commission and orders taking him farther away from the war than he had been before.

"Somebody's running guns to the west coast," Edgefield, of Army Intelligence, had said in essence. "Pacific Department's requested a man not known out there to go under cover and find out who and why and put a stop to it. I understand you have never been that far west."

"No, sir."

"You probably know there's a strong rebel sentiment in that area. It's particularly rampant now that the first six months of the war have gone so heavily against us."

"So I've heard, sir," Tracy had agreed. "How are the guns moving?"

"Some are going over the trails. That's how Pacific Department caught onto it. God knows how much there's been, since thousands of emigrant wagons go west every year. Just recently the Indians burned a couple that fell behind a train on the Humboldt. Underneath the household and farming equipment were several cases of guns. Short carbines and muskets, and probably stolen from the armory right here in St. Louis, where half the population, including the governor, is Secessionist."

Tracy whistled.

"The teamsters were killed by the Indians," the colonel resumed, "or doubtless they would have got rid of the evidence that tipped off the game. Being as far as the Humboldt, which runs across Nevada, the guns had to be going to the coast. That means that yet more munitions could be coming in by sea. You've got to get to the bottom of it, lieutenant. If we lose the West and its mineral wealth to the Confederacy, we're whipped."

Tracy did not doubt the gravity of such a plot, nor did he scoff at the idea that one existed. Colorado, Nevada and California held treasure enough to finance the war for the side that held them. Sentiment both ways was strong, although not so evenly balanced as here in bloody Missouri, with a majority in the West remaining loyal to the Union. But it seemed fantastic that such a grandiose scheme could be carried through to success.

Yet sobering afterthoughts had come since that brief interview. Much of the regular army had been pulled out of the West, a nondescript homeguard having been raised and rudely trained to replace it. If they could be provided with the necessary munitions, clever subversives might at least deprive the Union of a vast financial resource simply by closing all the overland trails. The Butterfield route through the Southwest had already been cut by the capture of Fort Bliss, at El Paso, by Captain Bayard and his Texans. If given the firearms, the Indians would be all too happy to sever the others. Thereafter a blockade of western ports by the Confederate Navy could seal off the whole vast region for the duration. . . .

The stage road had turned away from

the river, Tracy observed, and now slanted across a dead alkali flat toward another of the mountain strings that characterized Nevada. In a little over an hour the stage came to Desert Wells, another swing station, changed teams and ran immediately on toward the bare brown ranges. The country was not like the Colorado plains or the flat, mineral deserts of Utah, but a thousand valleys lying between digitate uprises. Tracy began to notice that the late November air was much colder, stirring now in a massive tow toward the timbered Sierras on the western horizon.

In late afternoon the Concord turned away from the old emigrant road that ran on past Carson City and over the mountains to California. Soon canyon walls pushed in on either hand and stamp mills appeared one after the other, with countless trailings dumps dotting the visible sidehills. Then shacks and mine headworks began to mix in, followed by a belt of better houses, and the Concord topped the grade and swung onto the main street of Virginia City, two thousand feet higher than it had been just a few miles back.

The old man had awakened and turned to look at the young woman beside him. "You stopping, lady, or catching the Pioneer?" She looked puzzled, and he added, "Lots of folks change here for 'Frisco and the California camps. The Central Overland stops here, and that's the Pioneer Stage Company's territory. What I mean is, I'm going on to Placerville. Help you make the change, if you like."

"Thank you, but I'm only going to Virginia City."

Drawing a crowd along with it, the stage wheeled up before the depot. Tracy swung down, and when he turned instinctively to help the young woman, she surprised him by readily accepting his hand. He walked beside her onto the sidewalk and through the press until they found a free space against the wall. She looked around, obviously slightly puzzled, and began to frown.

"It's on the rough side," Tracy said, "but it offers the best in the West. The nabobs can afford it. This town's already turned out a dozen or so millionaires."

"I know." For the first time she let her lips respond to him in a small smile.

"You expected to be met?"

"By my husband." Her voice was low-pitched but neither hard nor cold as her previous manner might have suggested. "He should have got my letter in time. I posted it in St. Louis."

He wondered what the odds were against her having seen him in uniform around St. Louis, which would interest her if she had also observed the exchange between him and the Fort Churchill corporal. He wanted to know more about her.

"You arrived there by steamer?" he asked.

"Yes."

"From Rebel territory, or is that using bad language?"

"I came down the river, not up. From Cincinnati. That's been my home since I was a child."

She had left St. Louis sometime after he did, for he had come by way of Denver and laid over there a short while so as not to proceed to Virginia City directly from the headquarters of the Missouri Military Department. He said, "Is your husband staying here or in one of the outlying camps?"

"Here. I've always addressed him at the International Hotel, at least. He was very much against my coming, but I didn't think he would — well, just ignore me." Again he saw the glint of temper in her lovely eyes.

"The International's the best in town, I hear. I'll escort you there, and we'll make inquiry. I'm Tracy Dalton, by the way. It's my first experience here, too. I've been in Colorado the past two years. Blackhawk, Georgetown, Central City."

"I'm Lorna Tremaine. My baggage?"

"I assume you'll stay at the International. They'll take care of it."

"Thank you. I think I would like an escort, at that."

The rough, noisy silver town did not frighten her as much as the fact of being caught in a far, strange place with her plans gone awry. She looked up at him briefly, then let him guide her along the thronged walk. Every other door seemed to open into a saloon or gaming house, but there were plenty of quieter, more useful enterprises. When they passed intersections, they could see the tilted, hill-girt plateau that fell away from Mount Davidson. The area was spiked with smokestacks rising above crowded clusters of surface buildings. The Comstock Lode was the marvel of the world, compacted in an area now completely covered by the town and its sister camp, Gold Hill, over the divide in the canyon the California road followed back to Carson River. There was plenty of reason, he thought, why Jefferson Davis would look upon it longingly.

The International was surprisingly stylish for so rough an environment. The clerk at the desk was polished and practiced, mistaking them for husband and wife and swinging the register about.

Tracy said, "The lady's husband is stopping here, I believe." He looked at her, lifting an eyebrow.

"Alan Tremaine," she said. "He's received his mail here since spring."

The clerk looked startled but covered it quickly. "Of course. He's one of our regulars, but he's been gone for the past few weeks. To Gold Hill." He laughed. "The one up in Oregon, I'm afraid. He has mining interests there, too, I believe. Your husband is a very busy man, Mrs. Tremaine."

"Yes," Lorna Tremaine answered and drew within herself again.

Tracy turned, thinking, too busy to meet a wife who's as beautiful a woman as I've seen. And Tremaine seemed to be something of a nabob himself, possessing scattered mining interests and maintaining permanent quarters at the town's most expensive hostelry. Aloud, he said, "I'm sorry, Mrs. Tremaine. I guess it's a matter of waiting till he shows up."

"Shall I have you shown to his suite,

madam?" the clerk asked.

"I suppose so," she said indifferently. She walked a little distance from the desk with Tracy, then added quietly, "I suppose I've got it coming. His last letter practically forbade me to come. He took it for granted, I suppose, that had ended it."

"But it didn't."

Her eyes met his. "I'm not an easy person to forbid, Mr. Dalton."

"Look," he said impulsively. "Nothing can be lonelier than a strange town, however large. Why not have supper with me?"

"They must have a dining room here. I'm sure I'll be perfectly safe." Then her pique showed in her eyes again, and she added quickly, "But why not? I haven't talked to anyone for a week."

"Your own fault."

"I'd have talked to you on the stage, but it would have let down the bars to all the others. I didn't feel up to it."

He was flattered, and when she had agreed to meet him in the lobby in half an hour he returned to the desk and registered, saying, "The lady'll want her luggage as soon as possible, and I'd like mine. Especially my razor."

"In just a few minutes, Mr. Dalton," the clerk promised.

The accommodations in which Tracy found himself were no suite but were wholly suited to his needs. Removing his coat, shirt and undershirt, he scrubbed away as much trail dust as he could while waiting until he could shave and bathe. The mirror gave back an unflattering reflection, for he had not been able to shave or even change his shirt since a night's stopover in Salt Lake City. It had been weeks since he had had time to have his hair trimmed. But Lorna Tremaine had been charitable, probably overestimating the damage the journey had done to her own appearance.

Turning away, he lighted one of the cigars he had denied himself while traveling, out of consideration for her, a fact she might have liked since the others had not been so considerate. Savoring the taste and fragrance, he withdrew from his trouser pocket the match case he had received from the corporal at the Fort Churchill stage station in exchange for his own. It contained a thin, rolled sheet of paper. . . .

"We've only had a summary report from Pacific Department," the colonel had said at Jefferson Barracks. "And you won't dare make contact with the military after you establish yourself on the coast. But Fort

Churchill has been instructed to prepare a list of those in the area who by attitude or actions might be suspected of subversion. Other posts are co-operating, so you might have California and Oregon names, as well." He described the method by which the list would be passed to Tracy at the desert station, which would be his last contact with the army. "If a subversive organization exists, you've got to get into it by ingratiating yourself with somebody already in. That'll take time and patience since, being a new arrival, you won't be trusted right off."

"I couldn't pose as another Confederate agent," Tracy reflected. "I'd have to have credentials and some knowledge of their underground apparatus. The first could be forged, but not the second."

"Nor can you pass as a Southern patriot, when your origin is proved by the way you talk. Anyway, the woods are full of those out there, already."

"I'd say, sir," Tracy offered, "that I'd do best as an outright soldier of fortune, out for what's in it for me."

The colonel nodded. "Which is why you were picked for the assignment. Your Colorado sojourn, I'm given to understand, was somewhat less than sedentary. I hear you can be a pretty rough customer. Lean on that. Live high, seek excitement and even violence, and lend the impression that you're strictly out for the main chance. They're much more apt to be taken in by that."

"High living costs money."

"You'll be supplied with funds before you leave. Spend lavishly and go broke fast."

"After which somebody offers me a chance to recoup?"

"It's something to work for, at least."

"What do I do for help if I reach a point where I need it?"

"Then you'll have to risk contact with the nearest military authorities. Good luck. . . ."

Now, long later and far removed, Tracy ran through the list and, when he had finished, had little more to go on than before, although there was a brief dossier after each name. But one thing was certain. Alan Tremaine's name was not on it. He was not sure why he had paid special attention to the names beginning with T.

Chapter 2

It was cold on the east slope of the Flowery Range, which separated Virginia City from the east desert, and the men unloading the mule train in the last daylight worked briskly. The packer who had brought the string down Six Mile Canyon watched moodily, a heavily constructed individual whose stance alone conveyed the impression of repressed restlessness. Now and then he spoke curtly, urgently, to one of the men wrestling with the stubby, corrugated tin cylinders with which they were disappearing into the shaft house of the mine.

The man beside him was stocky, with fair hair and a round, Teutonic head and face. He said with a slight laugh, "Well, that cleans up the surplus blasting powder from the Lady Luck. I'm sure glad to have it here."

"You ain't half as glad as I am, Groot." The packer had brought his string over the desert from Rogue River, a five day pack through country frequented mostly by the Modocs and Piutes. "And the rest's gonna be more ticklish yet."

"When're you starting on that, Hack?" Groot asked.

"Not till the boss says so, and he's got to wait for the right sign." Hack Hackett turned curiously, his alert ears having detected horseback travel before Groot heard it. "Turned off the canyon," Hackett reflected. "Somebody's comin' up here, Groot."

"Must be one of the boys. Wonder what's up."

Hackett barked at the men, "Hustle with them damned kegs. Don't bother to take 'em below. Just get 'em out of sight." He and Groot pitched in to help.

The mule string carried empty saddles when the approaching rider topped out of the draw and came through the gate of the mine yard. "It's all right," Groot muttered. "That's Pete Eaton. But something's got him excited."

The rider pulled up in a cloud of dust. He said, "Maybe we better go indoors, Oscar," and Groot nodded. Hackett followed them across the yard to the office. Groot entered last and closed the door.

"What's up, Pete?" he asked.

Eaton was breathless, testifying to the speed with which he had ridden and the excitement spurring it. "You know them army telegrams the woman sent word about? How they're plantin' a spy on us? Well, a corporal from the fort passed something to one of the stage passengers, all right. When Joe and me got the word, I hired a horse and fogged out to tell you."

Groot snapped, "Get a description of the passenger?"

"Just that he's young and tall. There was two like that on the stage, one a dude, the other a miner. Joe's tryin' to spot the right one and keep an eye on him while I ask you what to do."

"Tell Sanders to make sure who he is, then tail him every place he goes."

"Why not kill the bastard?" Hackett growled.

Groot retorted, "Not so fast, Hack. He was supposed to get a list from Fort Churchill. I'd sure like to know who's on it. But we can't do anything that'd prove they're barkin' up the right tree."

"They know they are," Hackett snapped. "Them guns we lost on the Humboldt proved it. And we can get along without a damned snooper around."

Groot ignored him, saying, "Pete, go back and tell Joe Sanders to watch his chance to stick up the bird. Knock him out, if he can manage, and get that list.

He'll have it on him. Too risky leaving it in his room. Take his money and watch, and it'll just look like someone jumped him. Plenty of that goes on all the time."

"What if Joe don't get a chance to jump him?" Eaton said.

"Then use his gun. But get the list."

Eaton went out to his horse and, a moment later, clattered out of the yard.

Groot shook his head. "Too bad it slipped with them burned wagons. Till then, the army and nobody else so much as smelled a rat. You ever hear the boss say when it's gonna happen?"

Hackett shook his head. "Don't think he knows any more about that than you and me. But one thing's sure. They won't risk anything that big till the worst of the winter's over. I'd lay my bet on February, sometime. Late enough there'll be good weather coming. Early enough the Army won't be looking for it yet."

"Makes sense." Groot lighted a lamp against the increasing darkness, picked up the pipe lying on the desk and began to pack it. "That gives us a couple more months of sweatin' blood."

"I need 'em. I'm supposed to work for other people, too, you know." Hackett walked to the door and yelled for the men to take the mules to the corral but to leave his saddlehorse. "Not that I ain't as jumpy as you. I wish we could light the fuse tonight. Things slip, and a man wonders what next. Well, I only got the stuff at Eureka to get to the Yuba River, then I can go back to J'Ville and haul the kind of freight that don't keep me lookin' over my shoulder for a while."

"Better tell the boss about this army fella. I hadn't even got wind of it when he left."

"Yeah, but you might see him before I do."

Hackett nodded and walked out into the darkness. The army man worried him, and he brooded about it while he rode up Six Mile toward the town. Coming onto the main street at its northern end, he turned left, hoping he could spot Joe Sanders. When he did, a few blocks later, Sanders was leaning against a lamp post outside the International Hotel. Hackett angled in to him.

Sanders looked at him in surprise because, except in emergencies, the men in the organization had as little to do with each other publicly as possible.

"He in there?" Hackett asked quietly, tipping a slight nod at the hotel.

"Yeah. Registered under the name of

Tracy Dalton. From Blackhawk."

"That's Colorado," Hackett mused. "Sure he's the one?"

"Gotta be. The other man his size on the stage wasn't exactly young."

"They wouldn't necessarily send a young 'un."

"Groot have somethin' more for you to tell me?"

Hackett shook his head. "I'm just curious. But was it me, I wouldn't be too particular. I'd kill and be shed of him."

"I'd feel safer that way, myself."

They exchanged brief grins, and Hackett rode on, a faint amusement still on his lips. He hadn't countermanded Groot's orders, but it wouldn't surprise him if things came out more according to his own ideas. Hackett was a great believer in direct action. Once one of his packers had taken to hitting the bottle, a man who knew too much to be trusted under such circumstances. Another time a rank outsider had blundered into camp and seen too much. Neither man had been seen nor heard from since. The boss knew about both instances and wouldn't be upset if something like that happened to this army spy. His neck would stretch, the same as anybody's, if the cat got out of the bag too soon.

Chapter 3

She exercised her woman's option and kept him waiting in the lobby for nearly half an hour. Tracy Dalton sat in a deep leather chair, bathed, shaved and dressed in a fresh suit. The town seemed as busy at night as by day, for the sidewalk beyond the windows displayed an endless parade. The lobby was full of people who came and went continually. The supper hour was about over, for they weren't entering and leaving the dining room in such numbers now. But when Lorna descended the stairs, it was well worth the wait.

A tub and access to her wearing apparel had worked a marvelous change, although she had been a striking woman in the rumpled, dusty suit and coat in which she had made the journey. He rose to his feet, and when she spotted him she smiled and kept walking to meet him, slim and lithe as a willow wand. Her attire was not lavish, but her sleek black hair glowed as if an expert dresser had attended to it, and her face and eyes looked fully fresh and rested. She had lacked the time for a nap, late as she was, which suggested a considerable reserve of vitality.

"Sorry," she said. "I wouldn't have blamed you for going ahead without me. I simply had to wash my hair."

"Don't women always?"

"After a trip like that they do."

"You're absolutely beautiful."

"Thank you. And you're even handsomer than I thought."

They entered the dining room and were given a good table where they could watch the street, although all he wanted to regard at the moment was Lorna. He was curious about her without wanting to pry and supposed she had the same problem until, when he had ordered, she disclosed a naive disregard for such niceties.

"Why aren't you in the war?" she asked.

It struck him that he had a right to ask the same thing about her husband, for he doubted very much that she would have married a man too old to serve. With a shrug, he said, "That's between North and South, and I'm a Westerner."

She cocked her head. "That's a distinction I never heard before."

"It's valid. This is new country. There's no reason why it should have colonial status."

"So a pox on both their houses?"

"That's right." At least she had stimulated a rationalization he might find useful again. And since she had started the prying, he added, "How about friend Alan?"

She sighed. "Maybe you've explained him to me, although he hasn't been in the West as long as you have."

"Did he come here to invest?"

"Not his own money. He hasn't much. But he represents people who do. I don't know much about it, really. He doesn't think women should bother their heads. But he's done all right for himself out here, as well as for his clients."

"Married long?"

She smiled ruefully. "Six months before he left, and I haven't seen him since."

The waiter began to serve them, and for a moment they were silent. Presently Tracy found himself as interested in the man she had married as those, if they existed, he had come to track down. For what purpose would a man leave a bride of six months as beautiful as this woman and even refuse to let her join him after a long separation? It couldn't be lack of funds, from what she had said. But it could be that his activity here was other or more than he had told her. Tracy was amused by his quick suspicion. Yet it had become his business to be skeptical of nearly everyone.

The meal would have been good under any circumstances. After those on the road, it seemed a feast. He was pleased that she ate with unabashed hunger, disdaining the dainty pretences that made so many women starve themselves. While she said little, he knew she was absorbed in thought, for now and then her brow wrinkled, and the expression of her eyes would change. He wouldn't have minded a bit had there been no Alan Tremaine, nor any other man in her life, to fill her thoughts until now.

Abruptly, she said, "What work do you do out here?"

He laughed. "The last man to tag me called me a soldier of fortune."

"How interesting," she said eagerly. "A gambler? Or do you sell whiskey to the Indians?"

"Well, I've done my share of the first, and not too badly, at that. I took a flyer in mining once, too, and made out quite well. For another stretch I rode guard on a stage between Blackhawk and Denver. I grew afraid of the temptation. Sometimes we hauled as much as fifty thousand a trip."

He had puzzled her, but he had to start building a reputation. This was practice, at least. And what he had told her was true, except for the temptation to steal and his reason for not being in uniform. There was a lot more in the same vein that was true, which had caused the Missouri Department to select him for this mission. The look it took depended on the slant a man gave it. Somehow he regretted that the one he must use with Lorna so strongly suggested irresponsibility and recklessness. He was sorry she had married a man who quite obviously did not appreciate her. He was sorry she had to wonder, as she must, if her husband really cared for her.

And don't forget, Dalton, he reminded himself, that she most definitely is married. And she's the kind that will stick to the last ditch.

They finished eating and separated at the foot of the stairs. But she lingered momentarily, saying, "Thank you. Even if we did travel days together, I feel I've had a very nice welcome."

"I'm glad."

He didn't press for another meeting. One was casual. More than one would be intentional, and it was folly to pursue what in good conscience could not be attained.

She smiled, spoke a soft, “Goodnight,” and ascended the stairs.

He was surprised to discover that it was only a little past eight o’clock. Tired though he was, he was not ready for sleep. Lighting a cigar, he stepped out to the street, not bothering to go back to his room for his hat. Although the wind had risen, it was not unpleasantly cold. The street had started to clear, finally, the motley population of the teeming town having started to sort itself out according to taste. The pleasure resorts were packed, the cribs on the street below were drawing business. Yet up the slope and down he could see the lighted windows of countless quiet homes. He noticed a number of soldiers, probably on passes from Fort Churchill.

Signs told him that the local newspaper called itself the *Territorial Enterprise*, and the main street was called “C” with admirable efficiency. The mines seemed to run night and day. There were a number of freight yards jammed with wagons that had groaned over the Sierras from California points of origin. He observed a theater called the Howard. The divided war sentiment was boldly proclaimed by the juxtaposition of the Southern Belle and Yankee Beauty saloons.

He was passing the latter when the door burst open to frame a pair of struggling men. One was huge and grasped the other by the nape of the neck and slack of the seat. The bouncer gave a heave, and the slighter man tumbled out on the walk ahead of Tracy.

"By God, Dink," bawled the big fellow, "I've warned you time and again not to start your Secesh harangues in this place! Next time I'll lock your jaw by bustin' it!"

The other sat up, looking injured and martyred, but Tracy had little interest in an open proselyte and passed on. He came finally to the end of C Street and was on the point of turning back when the impulse struck him to walk over the divide for a look at Gold Hill, a separate town about a mile away that was still part of the celebrated silver lode, surface gold having given it its name. The road ahead was deserted but easy to follow over what was hardly more than a ground swell. The wind increased. The area grew dreary, although there were scattered lights up the slopes on either hand. Large rocks abutted the road, and he had passed one when a voice punched at him.

"Wait a minute, Dalton!"

It came from a hind quarter, and he

swung about. A man had stepped out from the blind side of the rock. Tracy felt a shock of disbelief when he saw the pistol in the fellow's hand. This was no common footpad. His name had been used.

He said, "Well?"

"Hand it over."

"Hand what?"

"The match case."

As if an old mining drift had caved under him, Tracy felt himself sway dizzily for a second. All the doubt as to the reality and urgency of his assignment out here crumbled in that moment.

"Who are you?" he said harshly.

"Never mind that. Give it to me. Don't tell me you left it in your room. You wouldn't. Get it out of your pocket, and if you've got a gun don't try to unlimber it. I'll kill you. Hurry, damn you."

Recklessly reluctant, Tracy slid his hand into the side pocket of his trousers. "Why not? I can get a dozen more where it came from."

"Toss it over."

Tracy tossed the case, deliberately wide. With a curse, the thug swung himself slightly, trying to see where it landed. Tracy went forward in a bound. The gun roared, and he felt the sear of flame as he collided. His momentum carried the thug in a looping backfall to a sharp, cracking impact with the ground. The impetus somersaulted Tracy on beyond him, and when he scrambled up he was half dazed. Shaking his head roughly, he lurched back. The fellow lay motionless on the ground.

Tracy dropped to a hunker beside the still figure, puzzled. Then he realized that the inertia was more total than he had thought. The man's head lay on a flat rock imbedded in the sandy soil. There was no pulse in his wrist. Tracy muttered a soft, "Damn," while he considered it. The list could have been replaced, in a pinch, and he had gambled his life on the hope of choking a few facts from the fellow. He jerked up his head. Shouts came from down the road toward Gold Hill. He heard the sound of running men, who had been in earshot of the gun shot.

He groped on the ground for the case. Not that it was of much value, now, for his whole plan of secrecy and infiltration was obviously known. He found what he sought and slipped it into his pocket just as a party of three men loomed out of the darkness. They halted to stare at Tracy, who felt a sudden uneasiness. The dead man on the ground was young and dressed like a miner. They were apt to take the one standing over him, in eastern clothing, for the assailant. That was only jumpiness, he realized. They knew a murderer would have taken to his heels at the first alarm.

"Another of the bastards," one said. "You hurt?"

"Sound as a dollar."

"You did all right, and mebbe learned yourself a lesson. Folks around here know better than to go over this divide alone in the dark. Gettin' so's there's a holdup or something along here nearly every night. Better come along with us and tell the constable. Nobody'll run off with the carcass."

Two hours later, Tracy sat in the bare, pineboard office of the night police chief who ran, he had learned, the busiest shift in any twenty-four hours, half a dozen men being required to maintain a semblance of law and order in the vigorous town. He had made his report, stating only the fact of an attempted robbery, and waited until the body had been brought in, hoping his attacker could be identified. So far that had not happened.

"Have to wait till tomorrow," the night chief informed him. "I'll have the day boys check at the mine offices and see if anybody's turned up missing."

"The clothes," Tracy commented, "don't make him a miner."

"No, but it's likely he was just another young buck trying to make a raise for a good time. We get a lot of it. Payday's Saturday in the mines, and most of the boys are broke by Monday morning. The stinkpots get the bulk, and the girls on D Street cut a big chunk out of what's left."

Tracy nodded and got to his feet. "Well, let me know if he's identified. It shakes a man up, even if I didn't mean to kill him, I'd like to know if he left dependents."

"Sure. I admire your nerve, Dalton. But you were plain crazy to tackle him, no matter how much money you had on you. Don't crowd your luck so hard again."

Tracy walked out into the night and down C Street to his hotel, puzzled and depressed. A Confederate apparatus was indeed in business here, with a swift and deadly efficiency. It had known about him, perhaps from the time he left Jefferson Barracks, through a leak somewhere. That made it larger and better entrenched than even the military had supposed.

Why had they wanted the list so desperately, when he could get a duplicate from Fort Churchill? The answer had not come until he had reached his room, removed his coat and lighted a cigar. They had simply wanted to see it, themselves, to determine who, if any, of them were under suspicion. Except for the fluke that had turned the tables, he would have been the one to die on the divide. It would have looked like the work of a common footpad after his money.

That made him a marked man from this night on, known to enemies who were unseen and unknown to him. So he had the choice of reporting the development to the military and letting them try to send in a new man. Or he could accept the handicap, make no report, and continue with a conviction he had lacked before. He would have one advantage in that. They had not succeeded in obtaining the list. So no one involved in the subversive plot could be sure he was not suspect number one. The bright, disputatious energy that had filled Tracy on the divide slid through him again.

Withdrawing the list, he began to memorize it and the pertinent facts about each name. It was three in the morning when finally he burned the paper and dropped the ashes out the window to scatter on the wind.

Chapter 4

He could do nothing until the police had had time to identify the dead man, his best chance of gaining a fruitful lead. So he slept until midmorning. Then, after a quick breakfast, made his way along C Street toward the town jail. The vicinity hummed with life, black twists of smoke rolling away from the stacks dotting the lower landscape, white jets of steam rising among them. There were fewer people on the sidewalks and more vehicles in the street than there had been the night before: freighters, ore wagons, delivery vans and buggies.

A crowd was gathered before the newspaper office, scanning the bulletins for fresh news of the war. No matter how things were going, it would be good news to some, bad to others, in this divided town. So far the Secessionists were being favored. As if the disaster of Bull Run in the summer had not been enough, Washington itself was now in deep peril. In the mid-West the Union hold on the vital Mississippi was jeopardized. Union staff work was bad, its logistics worse, while the enemy had efficient, interior lines of communication and daring, imaginative leaders like Stonewall Jackson and Jeb Stuart.

The day shift had taken over at the jail. A sergeant with a calabash pipe stuck in his heavy jaws regarded Tracy jadedly.

"Had a little trouble on the divide, last night," Tracy told him. "Anybody identified the man who jumped me?"

"So you're the game bird." The sergeant looked more friendly and took the calabash from his mouth. "Yeah. He was a mucker or somethin' at the Silverhorn."

"That a saloon?"

"Mine down in Six Mile Canyon. Oscar Groot runs it. He says the fella'd only been here a few months and kept to himself. But one of the day boys remembered seein' him around. When we checked, that was it. He called himself Joe Sanders. Woman who runs the house where he boarded says he wasn't a high spender. Don't know what got him so hard pressed he went after money with a gun."

Sanders' name had not been on the list, but his motivation was clear to Tracy, although he didn't care to explain it. What interested him were the connections the man most certainly had, whether or not he had kept to himself. "I was worried about his leaving dependents," he said to cover his compelling interest.

"Nobody around here knows about 'em, if he had any. We turned the case over to the Washoe sheriff, since we found it had happened outside of town. He'll have to go through the rigamarole of an inquest to satisfy the law. Likely you'll hear from him about it."

"Help all I can. How far down the canyon to the Silverhorn?"

"Maybe couple of miles. It's one of Tremaine's mines. Only exploring, so far."

Sharply, Tracy said, "Tremaine? Alan Tremaine?"

"You know him."

"We have a mutual friend. He has other mines around here?"

"Nope, just the Silverhorn on the Comstock. Then he's got the Western Belle, over on the Yuba, and a couple more up in the Rogue River country. Enterprising fella."

"Must be. Thanks for the information."

"No trouble."

"You say Oscar Groot runs the Silverhorn?" That name had not been listed by Churchill, either.

"Not that it's runnin' yet. Tremaine's a

plunger. Buys up likely prospects from the discoverers, who usually don't have the money to develop 'em."

Tracy struck out for the foot of C Street and there turned right. The falling canyon cut him from view of the town, and the heavily traveled road slithered between rocky rises of bare, tailings-strewn hillsides. The original Comstock discovery had been made at the head of this canyon on the shoulder of Mount Davidson, and every square rod of ground fanning out from it had been probed for additional strikes. A number of hopeful prospects had been developed into mines in Six Mile, and many of the stamp mills for the mines on the overcrowded plateau were strung out down here, shaking the hills with their noise.

Yet Tracy strode along the edge of the road in growing preoccupation. Strong and complicated feelings stirred in him. The name of Alan Tremaine had recurred like the refrain of a song ever since he reached the Comstock. Backed by money whose sources even his wife did not know, he had acquired mines in three of the most prosperous districts of the coast: the Comstock, the Yuba, the Rogue. A man from one of them had tried desperately to obtain the list of subversive suspects supplied by Fort Churchill. He had known about the list within hours after it was passed at the Churchill stage station on the desert.

It was possible that the list was all but worthless, that the people actually engaged in the plot had conducted themselves in strict avoidance of talk or actions that would draw attention. He might have to compile his own list, but the fluke that had killed Sanders had given him a place to start.

Anybody could go on it, anybody at all, and he might as well open his mind to a thought he had been trying to avoid. Tremaine's beautiful, supposedly, neglected young wife had seen the contact with the army corporal, if not the actual exchange. She knew his name, in which hotel he was registered, could describe him. She had been late in meeting him for dinner, a delay he had supposed she had used for her grooming. She could have described him to somebody and had him trailed, guessing what had happened at the station. The thought was thoroughly depressing. He had liked her. Had she not been married, he would have been interested in knowing her much better.

Yet bits of the puzzle moved into place

with fearful persuasiveness. The mining districts in which Tremaine had interests adjoined each other. Tracy knew because he had pored over maps at Jefferson Barracks, realizing an intimate knowledge of local geography was indispensable. The Rogue Basin was mountain locked and isolated, communicating most openly with the desert on which lay the Comstock and the other Nevada camps of Star City, Silver City, and Unionville. The rich Yuba district was in the heart of the Sierras, just over the summit from the desert side and connected only by narrow canyons with the great valley of California.

The portent was awesome. A small, crack force of determined men might well seize the area and come into possession of the treasure heart of the West. They would have nothing but canyons and mountain passes to hold against all comers until reinforcements could land from the sea or come overland. There would be a practical sea-port in Crescent City, which was isolated from the rest of California except by sea yet was connected by a wagon road with the Rogue Basin in Oregon. Fort Bliss, at El Paso, Texas, had already fallen to a Confederate force and would make a good jumping-off place for an overland expedition. Meanwhile the subversive group already on hand would have recruited heavily from the large population of sympathizers throughout California, Oregon, and Nevada.

The guns found in the wagon burned by the Indians and the swift effort to obtain the list of names left no doubt there was such a movement. He could think of no better place for munitions and supplies to be stored than in a mine in each of the areas expected to be captured. Nor of a better cover activity for recruiting and training key men than a mine producing no ore but supposed to be exploring.

It was much less grandiose and far more practicable than he had supposed right up to his encounter with Joe Sanders. Yet he knew he had only a hypothesis, perhaps a flimsy one, with much he would have to prove or be able to prove before overt action could be taken. The first step was to see how others at the Silverhorn reacted to him.

He had walked over a mile when he came to a side road leading in from a draw to the left. A sign penciled on a piece of board pointed up the draw and said: SILVERHORN. He turned and climbed steadily for another half mile and then, at the top of the draw, came to the mine he sought. Comparatively, it was a small outfit. The yard was fenced, although the gate stood open, and when he passed through he saw a shaft and boiler house surrounded by half a dozen shacky little buildings. The yard was covered with ricks of mine timbers and cordwood fuel.

A saddlehorse with trailed reins stood in front of one of the shacks, which was labeled: OFFICE. He crossed to the structure, pushed open the door and stepped in. Two men sat staring at him, one at a desk, the other — who wore spurs — occupying a chair canted back against the bare wall.

"The name's Dalton," he said. "I'm looking for Oscar Groot."

They had never seen him, and if they knew his name and were disturbed by it, they did not betray the fact. The man at the desk said gruffly, "I'm Groot."

"I had a brush with one of your men last night. Joe Sanders."

"Oh, that. One of the camp police was out this morning. Sanders only worked here, Dalton. Didn't strike me as the type to try a stickup. But then men have surprised me before."

"The strange thing is, he wasn't after money. He demanded some kind of list he thought I had."

That time he got a reaction that made him hopeful that he had something here. The two exchanged glances, then Groot leaned forward. "A list?"

With a laugh, Tracy said, "That's what beats me. Talking like that and waving a gun. I thought he was crazy. So when he took his eye off me for a minute, I sloughed into him. I didn't mean to kill him. I only wanted to get that damned gun away from him. The barrel looked as big as a stovepipe."

The man in the cocked-back chair straightened his shoulders. "Why come here about it?"

"Curiosity about him, I guess. If he wasn't crazy, he must have mistaken me for somebody else. I've been wondering which ever since."

"Well," Groot said, "he was a mite queer. Notional, anyhow. Maybe he just got some wild idea in his head." He looked easier, and if these men had had a part in it, Tracy hoped he had confused them enough so that he might have a chance to throw them off his trail. "You ain't been around long, have you?"

"Just got in yesterday from Denver. From Blackhawk, actually."

The other men said roughly, "How come

you ain't in the war?"

"It's not my war."

They seemed to like that. Tracy turned to the door and added, before they could ask any more questions, "Well, if you can't tell me anything more about that crazy Sanders, I'd better be on my way. Much obliged to you."

He reached the main canyon and had turned back toward the town when a light wagon came rattling along behind. He slanted to the side of the road, but the vehicle pulled up when it came abreast.

"Want a lift?" the driver called.

He was scrawny, elongated, and wore a floppy hat. Lettering on the side of the hack bed read: GILPIN & MORRIS, GRO. & HDW., WE DELIVER. After the long siege of sitting on the overland stage, Tracy had felt the need of exercise. But the man's open, friendly manner won him. He walked around the wagon and swung up to the vacant seat. The wagon rolled on up the grade.

"Thanks," Tracy said. "It's a lot easier coming down this canyon."

"On shank's ponies, anyhow."

He looked garrulous, but Tracy wanted to ask the questions. "You an old Comstock hand?"

"Nobody's an old hand around here, mister. This camp's only been going a couple of years. But I landed here in the first rush."

"Then tell me something. Was the Silverhorn much of a prospect before Tremaine took it over?"

"Borrasca. Bottomed out. In case you don't understand mining lingo, that means busted as all hell."

"I know."

"But that don't mean much. Been more'n one outfit threw in the sponge within three feet of a big strike. Tremaine's spendin' money on the Silverhorn. Must know what he's doing."

The wheels rattled loudly on the rocky road, and Tracy was startled when a horse and rider appeared without warning on his left. The rider glanced at him in passing, and he saw it was the burly man who had been in Groot's office. The horse drew swiftly ahead, then disappeared around a turn in the canyon.

"Know that fella?" Tracy asked.

"That's Hack Hackett. He's around sometimes."

Hackett? That was another name Fort Churchill had not mentioned, persuading him anew he was forced to start from scratch. "What's his business?" he asked.

"Packing contractor for the different mines. Had a good thing before the wagon road was finished across the mountain. Serves camps off the main line now. Packs for Tremaine, sometimes. The man moves tools and supplies from mine to mine. Saves buyin' new for each one. The way prices are out here, it pays, I reckon."

"Hackett's headquarters here?"

"Last I heard, he was makin' his home base Jacksonville."

"That's up in Oregon."

The driver nodded. "Old placer camp that got a fresh start when they found quartz. There was a big strike at Gold Hill a while back. That's near there."

And where Tremaine's got another mine, where he's supposed to be right now, Tracy reflected.

He asked to be let down at the end of C Street, thanked the driver, and stepped into a short-order house for a bite to eat. The afternoon was half gone. There was one more bit of muddling he wanted to do. Returning to the hotel, he obtained the Tremaine door number at the desk, getting it readily since he had been with Lorna when she arrived. He ascended to the second floor and rapped. For a moment he thought she had gone out, then the door opened.

"Why, hello," she said, and smiled.

"All right if I come in a moment?"

She hesitated, then said, "Why not?"

He stepped into the elegantly furnished sitting room of a suite. She moved over decorously and closed the door to the bedroom, then turned back.

"That was quite an experience you had last evening," she said.

He hadn't expected any reference to it at all. "How did you hear about that?"

"They have a daily paper here. The management sent one up with my breakfast. My, you *are* the reckless western type." She was as open and friendly as she had been the previous evening after he had thawed her out. "How do you find the Comstock otherwise?"

"Well, not dull. But I've decided to take a look at California and maybe at Oregon."

"Oh?"

He couldn't tell whether her surprise resulted from his having slipped out of focus. Maybe she had only hoped he would be around for company to relieve what might be a long wait in this strange town.

"Frankly," he resumed, "I have a little money to invest. Think I told you I had luck with a mining adventure in Colorado. I'd sort of like to try my luck here. That is, somewhere on the coast."

"Too bad Alan isn't here. He probably could help you. How soon are you leaving?"

"Well, I understand the coroner, sheriff or somebody will want me at an inquest on that fellow last night. As soon as I can get that over with."

"Good luck." She offered her hand.

He left hoping that, if she was part of the subversive apparatus, he had made her as uncertain of him as he was of her.

He found the Storey County courthouse, where the sheriff informed him that in so clear-cut and routine a case his statement would be sufficient. He wrote it out, signed and left it. He got a seat on the Pioneer stage the next morning, and two days later was in the office of the Pacific Department Intelligence Officer, at the Benicia presidio.

This was Captain Traxler, a grey, stocky man who looked increasingly worried while Tracy recounted his experience since passing the Churchill stage station. He had helped set up the plan under which Tracy came west and was far from incredulous of his subsequent assumptions.

"Well, our list served a purpose," he said wearily. "It made them tip their hand."

"Since Joe Sanders hit his head hard enough to kill him."

"We deserved that break. The situation is much more acute than we thought. They would be ready to jump off."

"I rather doubt that they are, sir." The captain had given him a cigar that had gone out while he talked, and Tracy relighted it thoughtfully. "They're ready here, possibly. But it's my hunch that they'll have to wait on developments elsewhere."

"Such as?"

"Perhaps Captain Bayard had more in mind when he took Fort Bliss for the Confederacy than to cut the Butterfield stage road for us."

"As a matter of precaution, we've assumed that he did have. Fortunately, we've finally got our own intelligence set up. It's highly confidential, but the more information you have the better you'll be able to guide yourself. Bayard's being reinforced rather heavily. And we've just heard that Sibley's under orders to take command at Bliss. You've heard of Sibley?"

"Afraid not sir."

"He's another West Pointer who deserted us and went south at the start of the rebellion. All such officers have been given high rank in the Confederate army. He's now a brigadier general."

Tracy whistled. "Hardly an officer to command a little outpost on the west edge of Texas."

"But just the officer to command an operation against the whole West. We've assumed it's to be through New Mexico to the Colorado mines, then on to cut the central overland trail by taking Fort Laramie."

"Yet," Tracy reflected, "it could be a two-pronged drive, with another aimed at Nevada by way of the desert. Nothing stands in the way of either operation except a few undermanned posts."

"It's in the making," Traxler said moodily. "And it's a good bet the same kind of subversive apparatus had been set up in the Colorado mining towns. It's a help to know it, and we'll get busy. We might even have a little time, since the activity at Fort Bliss shows no great urgency. They're getting set, but the Rocky Mountain winters are rough. The weather around the Sierras isn't to be gambled with, either. That might give us a couple of months to get set to meet it, although I'm damned if I know what with. Every garrison out here's been stripped to a skeleton. The states and territories have raised militia, but only to guard the trails. They've had no training except in fighting the Indians."

"Which isn't bad training," Tracy commented.

"What do you propose to do next?"

"Well," Tracy said thoughtfully, "I've only got a supposition. But if it's essentially correct, I'd say the coast apparatus has a main base that's not on the Comstock. I'd put it at a more central location in the area they hope to seize. A substantial quantity of small arms and ammunition disappeared from the St. Louis Armory last spring, you know. Some, maybe all, of it came west during the emigrant season last summer and fall. By now it could have been distributed to the various mines I think are local bases. Again, maybe not. Large quantities of it could move in those huge overland schooners the emigrants use. Smuggling contraband into a congested mining region would be much more dangerous and time-consuming. I think that's where Hackett, the packer, fits in. He's set up for it, and I'm told he does a lot of work for Tremaine. In fact,

Tremaine makes a point of moving what's supposed to be excess supplies and tools from one mine to the other to keep his purchasing down."

"Knowing what we think we know now," Traxler mused, "it's almost glaring."

"They never expected us to wonder. The whole action is so unobtrusive, nobody would have except for the mischance of the Indians burning those wagons and Sanders getting killed. I understand that Hackett bases in Jacksonville. I think I will, too, for a while."

"You've probably made them uncertain of you, but they still won't trust you enough to let you work yourself in with them."

Tracy shook his head. "I've given that up. Likewise, I'm not wasting time on the list of suspects we had. I'm looking for a mine to buy. That will let me go to any camp I like, ask all kinds of questions and take my time. So with your permission, sir, I'll be on my way. I felt I had to risk this contact and tried to foul my trail doing it. But it isn't something I should repeat unless I'm forced to."

"I agree." Traxler offered his hand. "I'll see that every post in the affected area is alerted to the danger."

"I wouldn't trust the telegraph, anymore," Tracy told him. "They could have listening posts. The line could be tapped anywhere by a good telegrapher with a piece of wire, a handset and a pair of spikes. Or there could be a crooked employee in one of the regular stations. Possibly that's how it happened in my own case, although I'm afraid not."

Traxler's mouth showed a faint smile. "Afraid not? This Lorna Tremaine must be a damned attractive woman."

"That doesn't half describe her, captain."

"You realize that if she's engaged in it she's an enemy agent, the same as the men, and subject to the same penalties. Up to death by a firing squad."

"I realize it. I expect, if she's actively engaged, she also knows it."

The captain relighted his cigar, puffed up a white cloud of smoke, and was thoughtful for a moment. Then he nodded. "I think you've got the right approach. I served a while at Fort Lane, up there. I know a completely trustworthy man for you to get in touch with, and I think you should do it. John Ross. He's a colonel in the militia, although he hasn't been on active duty since the Indian war a few years ago. I saw him this summer when he came down to San Francisco. He's been in the Legislature, runs a prosperous farm, and he has mining interests. One of his associates is Henry Klippel, who knows as much about mining in that area as any man alive. They're natural men for you to seek out in connection with your desire to buy a mining property."

"That would help a lot, sir. I'll make a point of meeting them."

"Good. I'd say we've got till mid-February to get ready, that Sibley's moving out of Fort Bliss will be the signal to the local apparatus. Good luck again."

Chapter 5

Tracy had never seen a natural setting with the beauty and promise of the great basin of Rogue River. Coming off the winding grade of the Siskiyous, the California Stage Company's Concord spun out into Bear Creek Valley. Tracy, in a seat on the righthand side, saw opening east and north in wheeling agricultural plain dotted with the home of settlers. Beyond them rose the majestic Cascades that extended into Canada from the high Sierra, and on their eastern slope began the great desert that lay between these mountains and the Rockies.

The war seemed very remote here, for this was boom country of a more varied nature than the desert-born Comstock or the mountainous mining sections of California. The soil was amazingly fertile, the climate bland, the sidehills admirable pastureland. The initial placer boom had blended smoothly into hydraulic and quartz mining. All but zealots and corrupted traitors were too busy with their own prospering affairs to take more than a partisan, spectatorial interest in the great eastern struggle.

The stage road ran along the base of the mountain spur that jutted north from the Siskiyous and crowded against Rogue River, dividing its basin in halves, Bear Creek's counterpart to the west being the valley of the Illinois. All of it was settled now, although a long and bloody war with the Indians had been fought to win it, and various factors had given rise to a number of hamlets and towns.

The valley bottom made for fast traveling, and at the end of two hours the coach drew in sight of sprawling Jacksonville. The day was about spent, and this far north winter made its nearness plainly apparent in the crisp, clean air. The passengers, all men, began to stir in their seats. Tracy put a question to anyone who cared to answer it.

"What's a good hotel in this man's town?"

The man across said promptly, "Robinson House. Or Mrs. Cass' boarding house, if you're going to be around a while."

"Depends," Tracy said.

"Looking for a prospect?"

"That's right."

The town was at the edge of the foothills, sprawling out of the slope timber and spreading into the chaparral of a flat on either side of Jackson Creek. The stage came in on California Street, the principal thoroughfare, and stopped in the heart of town. The driver bawled, "Jacksonville! Meal stop for them as's goin' on!" All the passengers alighted, although the line ran on to Portland and some would presently leave with the stage. Tracy claimed his luggage when it came out of the boot, looking along the street and seeing something of the bustle of activity that characterized Virginia City. But this was a much older town, having sprung to life in the gold rush with the famed California camps. He found the Robinson House, registered, and by dark was established in a comfortable room.

He cleaned up and afterward got his pistol from a valise, a snub-nosed revolver he had chosen to carry in place of his easily recognizable service sidearm. He disliked keeping a weapon on him and hoped he had so beclouded his purposes he would have no immediate need of one, but he was not callow enough to entrust his life to that. He slipped the gun under the band of his pants, close to the left hip, and then descended the stairs and ate his supper in the hotel dining room.

Afterward he put in a couple of hours getting the lay and feel of the town. Oregon and California Streets, which bisected each other, formed its axes and were lined by the principal business establishments. He noticed a dozen or more stores that served the rich trading area, Bruner's brick-housed establishment being one of the largest. The livery stable was called the Arkansas, and he saw two bakeries, a bowling alley and a couple of blacksmith shops. The saloons were two or three to the block, some of them being located on side streets, and the sign on one of the better buildings announced that it was occupied by Beekman's Express Company and Bank. A dozen residential blocks paralleled California on either side, and at their outer edges lay the usual dumpy clutter of shacks, barns, corrals and wagon yards.

It was around ten o'clock when he stepped into a saloon and gaming house on California that called itself the Howling Wilderness. Miners, ranchers and townsmen lined the long bar and filled the tables and milled in the open spaces. He edged his way through these toward an archway in the rear, entering a less crowded room.

Chip stacks and the intent features of players and dealers told him this was the high stakes department. He saw an empty chair over by a wall, sat down and lighted a cigar.

In a matter of moments his attention had centered on the roulette table just across. There were half a dozen players, but their interest, like his, seemed drawn to a shaggy, standing man who obviously was very drunk. He was young, a strapping fellow, and had his profile to Tracy. He also had an impressive heap of chips in front of him. Tracy had watched it grow on three successive plays, and the wheel was spinning again. The fellow wore a slack, confident grin, but the faces of the others were stern.

The ball stopped, and the man raised a fist above his head, yelling, "Yippee!" Then he opened the hand in a negative gesture toward the croupier. "Huh-uh. Let her ride, Charlie. I've saddled me a pay streak, and I aim to ride her down!"

"Don't run your luck in the ground, Durnbo," the man next to him muttered.

Durnbo answered with a reckless laugh. "Hell, man, I can't lose! Spin her, Charlie, and let me show 'em!"

Perhaps Tracy was the only one aware of

two men standing at the wall across from him, beyond the game and watching it with the alert energy of falcons. They were shabbily dressed, their hard faces darkened by whiskers, and both showed the stains of some long trail. They exchanged glances when Durnbo won his wild gamble again, then one of them left.

In a clipped voice, the dealer said, "That's all, Ridge. We don't roll drunks in here."

Truculently, Durnbo said, "Who's drunk?"

"You're tighter than a tick, and you don't gamble like this usually. One or two more plays, and you're goin' back to your cattle ranch broker than when you hit town with your beef."

"It's my money." Durnbo teetered on the edge of belligerence for a moment, then reason seemed to work its way into his drink-muddled mind. He shrugged. "You're a good egg, Charlie. If you didn't run a straight game, I'd of been cleaned already. So I won't break it for you." He wagged a finger. "But I could. I could stand here beatin' you till daybreak comes and I head back to the desert."

"Cash in," Charlie said gently. "And let Sam put the money in the safe for you till tomorrow."

"Got to get home, and I'm leavin' come light." Durnbo stuffed the chips in his pocket, turned and staggered out of the room.

A man laughed in relief and said, "Never seen him buck the tiger that way before. Or get his snoot so full."

"Been on the desert all summer," Charlie said. "And he'll be there again all winter. Can't blame him for cuttin' loose his wolf."

"How much he take you for?"

"Couple of thousand, anyhow."

The game resumed, and Tracy would have forgotten Durnbo had not the saturnine-faced man who had remained there to watch strolled off toward the archway. Nobody else seemed to notice. Tracy got to his feet, dropped his cigar in a cuspidor, and went along in the rear. The whiskery individual had stopped as if to watch a mild card game in the outer room, but he was positioned where he could see Durnbo, who was cashing in. He followed when Durnbo stepped out to the street. Tracy hesitated a moment, not sure his imagination had not got the better of him. Then he went outside to discover that Durnbo was the only one of them in sight on the now quiet street.

The big man was weaving along California, a couple of blocks to the east, and he turned off at the end of the block he was in. Tracy stood rubbing his jaw, then walked in that direction, realizing he would himself look suspicious if anybody was watching him. The street into which Durnbo had turned was dark, running between the sides of buildings fronting California and the next street over. Tracy followed it until he came to another intersection. There were no more lighted windows to help him see, but the street leading east seemed to meet the edge of town at the end of a brushy, nearly vacant lot. There probably was a feed corral down there somewhere, where Durnbo had left his horse. He should be warned against leaving town in the night or sleeping at the corral until it was light enough to travel in some degree of safety. Tracy hurried after him.

He had taken only a few steps when a figure loomed out of the darkness just behind Durnbo, with another right behind it. Tracy yelled and went forward in a run, seeing Durnbo haul around just as the pair of trail wolves leaped onto him. They had heard him and were hell bent to finish the job fast. Tracy saw in dismay that one had his hand up to strike with a knife. He whipped out the pistol and fired a shot, not daring to aim at the desperadoes for fear of hitting their victim. Durnbo's leg lashed out, and he kicked off the man with the knife. The other was trying to pin his arms. Durnbo wrenched away from him, and the pair gave it up, cutting off into the brush.

Tracy hurried on up. He could hear the two thugs crashing through the brush, but his purpose had been to save Durnbo rather than to capture them. He had drawn attention to himself in Virginia City in connection with Joe Sanders, and to repeat that here might create awkward complications.

Panting, Durnbo said uncertainly, "Who — who are you?"

"Just happened to see those two trail you out of the Howling Wilderness and followed. Mister, that pair didn't mean to leave you alive."

"Seen the knife. Thanks."

"Just don't undo it," Tracy snapped, "by inviting them to try it again. I'm Tracy Dalton. Come back with me to my hotel. Put your money in the safe, take a room and sleep it off before you try to go home."

"Yeah, you're right," Durnbo said. "They got their wind up, and they ain't gonna discourage easy."

The short, deadly fight had sobered him, but he was unsteady. Still not easy about the situation, Tracy hurried him back along the route he had followed out, breathing more easily when they reached California Street. Ten minutes later he saw Durnbo into a room down the hallway from his own, with the money locked up downstairs.

Lingering a moment, Tracy said, "Where's this cattle ranch of yours?"

Durnbo grinned. "Cow camp," he corrected. "In the Lost River country, not far from Tule Lake."

"Thought that was Indian country."

"Sure is. The Modocs. But they won't bother a man if he treats 'em right, which I do. Main danger is from the Piutes that stray up from Nevada. That breed's coyote mean."

Tracy liked the brashness of the man. "Been out there long?"

"Me and my pardner took out three hundred steers last spring. Just brought in fifty head to sell, fat as butterballs on bunchgrass. It's great cattle country. Pretty soon there'll be ranches all over the place." His features darkened. "My pardner's still out there, and that's why I'm doubly grateful to you, Dalton. It was partly his money I risked in that game." He grinned dreamily again. "But it was sure a sweet run of luck."

Dryly, Tracy said, "Yeah, but if I were you I wouldn't try it more than once to the lifetime. You must be located somewhere close to the emigrant road."

"A little north of it. You gonna be around here?"

"I'm looking for a mine to buy. If I find something, I will be."

"Well, if I ever get a chance to pay you back, I sure will."

"Not the same way, I hope," Tracy said and laughed. He would have liked to question Durnbo more closely about traffic over the trail from the east, particularly in connection with the Indians and whether he had seen any signs of them acquiring guns or even whiskey. For it had occurred to him that the Confederate apparatus might plan to use them and their natural antipathy toward the white people to keep the trail garrisons diverted and tried up. But he knew nothing about Durnbo except by snap judgment and didn't want to start him wondering. He offered his hand, which the man took gratefully, and left.

He was the first in the dining room when

it opened, the next morning, and when he had eaten his breakfast he walked down to the Arkansas Livery and asked for a rental horse for all that day and possibly the next.

"Want a look at Gold Hill," he explained. "There's a stage makes the round trip every day," the hostler said. "Not that I'm tryin' to talk myself outta some business."

"I'll want to look around out there, so I might as well pick up a horse here. I understand Henry Klippel's connected with one of the bigger mines out there."

"The biggest. You know Klip?"

"I was advised to look him up. He live out there?"

"Nope. He stays out there a lot, but he keeps his family here in J'Ville."

"See him one place or the other."

Tracy rode out Oregon Street, and presently the road began to climb, swinging over the brow of a hill. As he gained elevation, he caught a splendid view of the great valley, crisply cool in the early winter sunlight. It felt good to be in a saddle again, and he rode at a brisk trot, descending to the valley floor after a time and passing a settlement that called itself Willow Springs. Not long afterward he could see Fort Lane off to his right against Rogue

River. Once it had been a considerable post, but it was now reduced to a skeleton housekeeping force, while its duties had been taken over by a company of militia. This contingent occupied Camp Baker, on the old emigrant road and east of Jacksonville.

He recognized Oregon's Gold Hill from the inevitable prospects that began to dot the slant above him. The town and most of the mines were on the other slope, above the little valley of Kane's Creek. Presently he saw a gap ahead, which the road entered. A little after eleven o'clock he came down to Kane's Creek near its mouth, and to the town.

It was hardly more than a hamlet, jerrybuilt and raw new. Most of the mines ran their own boarding houses, while the town served travelers, prospectors, the Chinese working over the old gravel bars, and a considerable agricultural settlement. There were rigs and saddlehorses along both sides of the road, attesting to the humming activity of the area. Tracy saw a large store, with a blacksmith shop next to it. Across the road was a hotel with a stable in the rear, and there was a saloon in the separate building next door. A dozen or so houses completed the inventory.

Odd place for Alan Tremaine to hang out so much, he thought, considering the fancy suite he keeps rented in Virginia City. His next move was to find out, if possible, why that was.

Chapter 6

The saloon seemed a good place to make inquiries, and Tracy angled in, dismounted and tied his horse at the hitch rack. Stepping across the porch, he entered the establishment to see another of the countless bar and card table setups he had frequented all over the frontier. The town seemed to have plenty of idlers, for there were a couple of card games going. Other men strung themselves along the bar in twos and threes, engaged in conversation. Tracy moved into an open space at the bar and instantly pricked up his ears.

"I'll have to wait till Hack gets back," the man on his right had said.

The man beyond said impatiently, "When's he gonna get in? Been gone three weeks, now."

"You know how Hackett racks around. But it ought to be any day."

Tracy realized they were talking about the packer he had encountered in Groot's office at the Silverhorn. The man was still away from here, and it seemed unlikely that Groot would have believed it necessary to send a warning to Tremaine by mail when he was himself unsure of the situation. That made it safe to look around a little more openly here than he had expected. The barkeep moved up to him, and he ordered a whiskey. The pair on his right went out.

"Man get oats for his horse around here?" Tracy asked the bartender. "And a meal for himself?"

"Nan's place."

"Nan?"

"Nan Bollinger. She runs the hotel. They'll take care of your cayuse, and they serve meals."

"Thanks. Where's all the mining?"

"Up on the sidehill. Looking for work?" The bartender glanced skeptically at Tracy's uncalloused hands.

Tracy shook his head. "Might be interested in a property, though, provided I found something attractive."

"Another one of them, eh? You from Nevada?"

"Colorado. Blackhawk, Georgetown, Central City."

"Mine there?"

"That's right."

Others were listening, although nothing

indicated that it was with more than idle curiosity. A man grinned and said, "There's a hundred prospectors around here, mister, who've got a gopher hole to sell somebody."

Tracy smiled knowingly. "Yeah, but I'm after a mine. How do I reach the Gold Hill?"

"Think you can buy that mine?"

"I want to see Henry Klippel."

He saw that the name drop had impressed the listeners. "Dunno if he's out here right now," the bartender said. "Lives in J'Ville."

"If he isn't here, I can see him there. No hurry."

Tracy finished his drink, dropped a coin on the bar and went outdoors. Leading his horse, he walked over to the stable and ordered it fed. The hotel dining room was already serving the noon meal, although it was still short of twelve. He ate, and when he passed out through the lobby, a woman stood beyond the desk. He glanced at her with immediate interest, for she was very attractive, out of the prime of girlhood but not yet matronly. She had chestnut hair, he observed, and large brown eyes that appraised him shrewdly.

"The dinner'll be a dollar," she said.

"Well worth it, Miss Bollinger. Or is it Mrs.?"

"Miss. Who told you my name?"

He laughed. "Your hostelry is more famed than you seem to know. I was told to be sure and have a meal at your place."

That pleased her. "You staying a while? If so, you'd better register now. We have to turn 'em away every night."

"Depends on whether I can see my man. Henry Klippel."

"Klip? He's up at the mine. That's where he stays when he's out here."

"How about Alan Tremaine?"

Her eyes narrowed. "You know him, too?"

"No, but I traveled with Mrs. Tremaine coming west. She said he was here temporarily."

"Mrs. Tremaine?" she said puzzledly. "His mother?"

"His wife."

Her eyes turned cold. "Somebody pulled your leg, mister. He isn't married."

For a moment they stared at each other, feeling some strange, concerted shock. She had knocked his picture of Lorna out of kilter, as he knew he had hers of Alan. He said quietly, "Where's he staying?"

"Here. But he won't be in till evening."

"What's his mine?"

"The Lady Luck, up on the hill."

"Well," he said lightly, "If Klip's out here, I'd better make sure of a bed tonight."

He registered but declined to inspect the room she assigned him, saying he would be back at suppertime. She was still troubled, and he was sure she would like to question him more closely about the woman he had mentioned. He headed for the stable wondering if Tremaine had posed as a single man out here. The clerk at the International in Virginia City, he recalled, had been surprised when Lorna identified herself. That seemed more plausible than the possibility that she had misrepresented her status.

He spent several hours riding along the network of roads that connected the mines. The Gold Hill was easy to identify by the scope of its operations, and several locations in its immediate environment seemed busy and prosperous. Yet he had scarcely more than a tourist's interest in these, since the Lady Luck was the main target of his curiosity.

It was outside the concentrated area, on the open brow of the big hill where it broke in a gap through which flowed

Rogue River. The Lady Luck was no more impressive on its surface than the Silverhorn had been, although this was an adit and tunnel mine, unlike the deep shaft operations in the silver country. The small, cluttered yard appeared deserted, and the road Tracy had followed ran on by. A badly lettered sign on a piece of board pointed on and said: YELLOW JACKET.

That length of road showed use, and he went on, for it was not his intention to make an open visit to the Lady Luck. And he was surprised when, just around the first turn, he came to the entrance of a dinky mine. A single shack stood beside the adit, and it, too, was labeled: YELLOW JACKET. On the other side of the timbered opening was an *arrasta,* the crude device by which one-horse mines crushed their ore. Rusty car tracks ran out of the adit to the arrasta, but their surfaces showed they were in use. He saw fresh waste on the dump.

After a moment's thought, in which no one appeared on the surface, Tracy swung his horse about and started down the trail. He was ready finally for a talk with Klippel who, he learned at the Gold Hill mine, was down at the stamp mill on Kane's Creek. Tracy followed the road used by the ore wagons and, at the foot of the grade, came to the mill. Momentarily the noisy stamps were idle while the amalgam table was cleaned, and Klippel was watching this.

When the man was pointed out, Tracy was surprised to see that he was little older than himself, despite his standing in the mining industry. He was slender, with an oval face and a prominent, straight-ridged nose, and he wore a moustache and carefully trimmed goatee. There was a look of steeliness to him, but his manner was genial.

"Friend of Bart Traxler's, eh?" he said, when Tracy had introduced himself. "I remember him well . . . What can I do for you?"

"Not much, maybe," Tracy admitted. "Again, maybe a lot. Any place we can talk in private?"

Klippel glanced at him shrewdly. "Sure. Come on." He led the way out of the mill and across its yard to a shack that appeared to be an office but was deserted until they entered. Klippel shut the door and looked inquiringly at Tracy.

"I've taken the liberty of dropping your name around here," Tracy told him. "I'm supposed to be in the market for a mining prospect. Actually, I'm in Army Intelligence, out of Jefferson Barracks. First Lieutenant Tracy Dalton, to be exact. Captain Traxler suggested that I take you and Colonel Ross into my confidence. For obvious reasons I don't carry credentials, but you can check with the captain by post. I hope you will."

"Depends," Klippel drawled, "on what you want, Dalton."

"Information and help. There's strong reason to fear that a plot exists to seize the coast for the Confederacy in concert with a move against the Rocky Mountain region from Fort Bliss, Texas. If we're right about it, one of the bases for the coast effort is right here."

"What?" Klippel said, blinking.

Swiftly, Tracy explained the probable existence of an apparatus set up to seize the treasure center of the west, particularly that of the coast, a mountain-girt area that would lend itself to easy defense once it had been captured. While he talked, he watched the incredulity fade out of Klippel's lean face to be replaced by dismay and shock.

"Well," Klippel said, when Tracy stopped talking, "Secessionists come a dime a dozen around here. Some are important people, but nobody worries about

’em because, mainly, they just run off at the mouth. But with skilled leaders and arms and a fair chance to carry the day, some of them would go along with a scheme like that.”

Tracy nodded. “We’ve got to deprive them of the opportunity, and God knows whether we’ve got months, weeks or days to do it in. We can’t arrest the ringleaders until we’re sure of them and that we know who all of them are. They’re too easy to replace. Arms and ammunition are a different matter, much harder to bring in and hide in quantity. Yet we can’t just seize Tremaine’s mines. I may be wrong about them being used for storage and ruin my chances of discovering the real caches in time.”

“Well, it makes sense out of him holding onto the Lady Luck. It isn’t earning him a dime. A lot of us have wondered where he keeps the money to keep going.”

“I’d say from Richmond.”

“Wouldn’t be surprised.” Klippel’s shock was giving way to anger. “Well, they won’t get away with it, Dalton. I hit this country when I was nineteen, ten years back. John Ross was here ahead of me, and most of the others, like Cornelius Beekman, weren’t far behind us. Don’t think we’re gonna sit back and let a bunch of Johnny Rebs take over."

"Good. I've got to get into the Lady Luck for a look around. If I'm right about it, there's no chance of slipping in from the surface. They're guarding that entrance day and night. I rode by there a while ago, and while I was there I had an idea. You know the Yellow Jacket?"

Klippel nodded. "That's old Abe Jewett's mine."

"I noticed that it lays back to back with the Lady Luck, and at nearly right angles."

"It does. Abe staked the claims. He owned the Lady, too, till he sold it to Tremaine. His boys went off to war. Four of them. The Lady was too much for him to work alone, so he sold out. Kept the Yellow Jacket to occupy himself and earn bacon and beans. Tremaine's been developing the Lady on a much bigger scale than Abe could afford."

"I'm wondering," Tracy said, "if there's any place where the two mines connect underground. I know adjoining mines sometimes do hook up to improve their ventilation."

"Neither was big enough in Abe's day to need that. And if you're right about Tremaine, he wouldn't want any such connection."

"Which army was it Jewett's boys joined?"

Klippel chuckled. "You ask Abe that question, and he'll bend a pick handle across your head. He come from Illinois, and the call for volunteers had scarcely reached here when the boys were off for home to join up. Abe would have gone, too, if they'd have let him."

Tracy grinned. "Maybe if he knew what we think, he wouldn't object to a drift being run from the Yellow Jacket to the Lady, sort of on the quiet."

"By damn," Klippel said musingly, "it could be done, and he'd be the man who would and could do it. He knows both layouts. Some of the existing drifts probably aren't too far apart. You want me to feel him out?"

"That's what I had in mind. Has he got the crew for it?"

"Only four or five men, but they could handle it. They're all reliable. Abe wouldn't stand for a Secesh around him all the time."

"If he'll do it, and let me get into the Lady in secret, I'm sure the government will reimburse him for the cost."

"If you convince Abe that Tremaine's a Reb, he won't want reimbursement. I'll see him."

"Fine," Tracy said. "He'd have to connect with an old drift in the Lady, of course. In an area Tremaine's force doesn't frequent."

"Give Abe a chance to match wits with a Reb agent, and he'll do all right. But it'll take time. Maybe weeks."

"I know," Tracy agreed. "And I think it better for me not to hang around while it's being done. Now, I don't want to visit nothing but areas in which Tremaine has interests. Since I'm supposed to have come to you for mining advice, where'd you suggest I go?"

"Take a look at the Steamboat country. That's way up on the Applegate, and he has nothing there. Then you could catch a stage for Kerbyville and Waldo and look around in the Illinois. Tremaine's got a mine at Waldo called the Gold Star."

"I've heard that, and I want a look at it. Waldo's on the wagon road from Crescent City. If anything's been smuggled in by sea, the Gold Star might be the first depot for it, with later distribution out of there."

"Could be," Klippel agreed. "It's damned isolated. And Hack Hackett packs over that trail a lot, too."

Tracy held out his hand. "I'll be going, and thanks a lot. I suggest that you post

Colonel Ross and also whoever's commanding the militia company at Camp Baker."

"That's Lindsay Applegate, an old timer."

"Good. Tell them there'll probably be two warnings. Indian trouble out here to keep the trail garrisons diverted, and some kind of action by General Sibley out of Fort Bliss." He turned toward the door, then halted a moment. "It would be quite understandable, sir, if you checked up on me with Pacific."

"If you're that willing, I don't reckon it's needful. And I think I can promise Abe'll have something for you when you get back."

"And one thing more. Can you suggest anybody at Waldo I can confide in? Somebody who could keep an eye on the Gold Star and has an idea of what might happen?"

"Chance McCabe," Klippel said readily. "County sheriff over there, and he's used to keeping his eyes open and mouth shut."

"You acquainted on Yuba River?"

"Some. Tremaine's mine there is the Western Belle in the San Juan neighborhood. Powerful rich, quartz and placers they're working with hydraulic giants. It's to gold what the Comstock is to silver."

"He making any money there?"

"I just wouldn't know about that." Klippel laughed. "But Jeff Davis would sure want that country included in the haul."

Tracy rode back to the town feeling that he had made progress. John Ross had military experience, knew the country and its inhabitants, and was quite capable of organizing a defense against a Secessionist uprising, should things reach that point. That would let him concentrate on his desperate effort to hamstring the movement before it could happen. If Klippel and Abe Jewett could get him into the Lady Luck in secret, he might make considerable headway with that.

He was through here for the time being, but since he had engaged a room at Nan Bollinger's hotel he decided to spend the night in Gold Hill in hopes of a casual encounter with Tremaine. Reaching the village, he left his horse at the stable, went on to the hotel to find the lobby empty, and rang the bell.

A door opened, and through it came Nan Bollinger. Her look of inquiry turned into one of recognition, and she said, "Want your key?"

"Please."

She gave it to him, standing erect and graceful beyond the desk. "Well, did you buy a mine?"

"Not this trip. Klip suggested that I take a look at Steamboat."

"That's in the wilderness."

"Don't care what's above the ground, if what I want's beneath."

"Leaving in the morning?"

"That's right."

"Well, supper's at six."

Nodding, he turned toward the stairs.

The room was plain but clean, and his watch showed him it was a couple of hours until suppertime. He lighted a cigar, then took off his coat and boots and stretched out on the bed. He wondered why a woman as personable as Nan Bollinger was still single, and recalled her quick, vehement denial that Tremaine was a married man. He would have to see Tremaine before he could speculate on whether she had been beguiled by him. And, possibly, badly deceived.

He had finished the cigar and dozed for a long while when a rap on his door aroused him. The light in the room had dimmed and, thinking he had overslept and was being called for supper he said, "Yes?"

"Like to see you a moment, Dalton," a man's voice replied.

It was not one he recognized and, puzzled, he climbed to his feet, walked over and opened the door. A man about his own age but much better dressed stood in the hall. He had no hat, which suggested he was from within the hotel.

"I'm Alan Tremaine," he said and offered his hand.

"Come in."

Tracy shook hands briefly, stepped aside while the man passed through, then shut the door. Tremaine walked to the window, then turned around and smiled. He was dark, smooth-shaven, the type physically that women would like. Tracy watched him with wary reserve, curious about his purpose and thinking that he would have disliked him had he known nothing about him at all. There were flaws in men women never suspected until too late, just as women could read their sisters with a sharper eye than men.

But Tracy sensed no present hostility in Tremaine, who seemed more embarrassed than anything. "Might as well get to the point," the visitor said finally. "Nan — Miss Bollinger tells me that you traveled west with a Mrs. Tremaine."

"Between Salt Lake and Virginia City. She called herself Mrs. Alan Tremaine, incidentally, but Miss Bollinger assured me that you have no wife."

"She's my wife." Tremaine made a frustrated gesture.

"If her name's Lorna, she is."

"I had no idea she'd be so persistent."

"She said she wrote you from St. Louis that she was on her way. She seemed quite let down when you didn't meet her."

Irritably, Tremaine said, "I got the letter. And I telegraphed her immediately forbidding her flatly to come. I supposed that she'd turned back until Nan mentioned that you had seen her."

"Perhaps you've been alienated?"

Tremaine shook his head. "This country isn't for women like Lorna, that's all."

"Your diggings in Virginia City," Tracy drawled, "looked liveable."

"I'm giving them up. I'm making this my headquarters. I have to move around a lot, Dalton. She'd be alone a great deal in a raw, rough country where she has no friends."

"I see." Where also, Tracy reflected, she might learn too much. Where she might possibly be jeopardized by the fight you're busy arranging.

Tremaine smiled awkwardly. "You're curious, naturally, about Nan. To be frank, I haven't been completely candid with her, Dalton. I fancy you gathered that. A man gets lonely. Since I understand you've been on the frontier a while, yourself, I expect you know how it is."

"Indeed I do. I probably complicated things by letting the cat out of the bag."

"No matter. It was getting to where Nan had to know. Especially since my wife has chosen to ignore my wishes in the matter."

"I don't think she got your wire," Tracy told him. "She expected to be met in Virginia City."

"I assure you I'd have been there had I dreamed she was coming. And I'm leaving for there in the morning."

"To send her home?"

"It's too close to winter for me to start her back over the plains. And I suppose there's no use trying to persuade her to return by sea."

"She told me she's a hard woman to forbid." Tracy was enjoying the man's discomfort, for he sensed a strong pride in him. "I'd suggest, Tremaine, that you consider her wishes and let her remain with you. Although not in Gold Hill. Jacksonville has good accommodations and seems a pleasant town."

Thoughtfully, Tremaine said, "Nan tells me you're interested in mining properties."

Tracy laughed. "Not in any large way. But I was successful in a venture in Colorado and have a little money to play with. I'm taking a look at the Steamboat country at Henry Klippel's suggestion."

"They've good prospects there." Tremaine walked to the door, then hesitated to add, "Please understand, Dalton. My wife's a wonderful woman, and I'm completely devoted to her."

"Of course. If I have the pleasure of meeting her again, I will say nothing about Gold Hill."

That was what Tremaine wanted assurance about. He made a slight bow and left.

Tracy combed his hair and put on his coat, for noise belowstairs told him that supper was in progress. He felt an elation that came from much more than the fact that Tremaine, so far, had received no warning about him. It had begun to look as if Lorna might be in complete ignorance of her husband's real purpose in the West.

Chapter 7

Tremaine's fingers trembled while he knotted his cravat, and he kept glancing over the shoulder of his reflected image toward the interior door of his room. Beyond this door was the small parlor and the bedroom used by Nan Bollinger. He wondered how many besides her and the hotel help knew that this room, regularly assigned to him in his long stays in Gold Hill, had once been a part of her private quarters and was still connected with it by a door left unlocked when he was here. Secrecy in matters of that nature had scarcely concerned him until Nan had confronted him stormily, the evening before, with what Dalton had let drop in his innocence. Now Tremaine was making an early morning start for Virginia City. He had not decided what to do about Lorna, but he hoped he could get away without another scene with Nan.

He had scarcely concluded the wish when the door he watched moved. As the gap widened, he saw Nan's face, then she gave a toss of her head and came in.

"Well, I don't suppose I'll see much of you from now on," she said.

"Nan, I told you —"

She lifted her hand. "I know. I took too much for granted in assuming you were fancy free. I should have pinned you down."

"I'm not the first man —" he began angrily.

"I know. Forget it. Does Lorna know what you're doing out here? I mean besides using a private entrance to another woman's bedroom?"

He hesitated, then shook his head. "No, and she's not going to find out."

Nan smiled. "She's loyal to the land of her birth?"

"I don't like that way of putting it, but she doesn't share my sentiments."

The smile became a laugh. "Your sentiments. Really, Alan. You might fool some of the local cotton pickers about that. But not me. Your sympathy doesn't lean North or South. It doesn't even lean. It rests firmly on Alan Tremaine."

"I'm risking my life for what I consider a worthy cause."

"For what you expect to make you a big power on the coast after you've delivered it to Jeff Davis."

Bitterly, he said, "I was a fool to confide in you."

"But I steered you to the kind of people you had to line up. Remember? Not that I share your sentiments, either. I did it because it pleased you."

He whirled toward her. "Look here, Nan. You're bitter, and I can't say I blame you. But don't let it turn you vengeful. You don't know enough to do any real damage. And doing just a little damage could prove very costly to you. There are men involved besides me who're risking their lives."

She pursed her lips. "That's a threat, of course."

"It's a warning not to get out of line. There've been a few people who have, one way or another. They're not around anymore."

Her face sobered. "I don't intend to get out of line."

"That's a noble resolution, and I advise you to keep it." The harshness of his words seemed cruel after what they had shared. More gently, he said, "I never dreamed that my wife would ignore my protests and come out. Believe that, Nan. I didn't and don't want to hurt you."

"Do you love her?"

"Yes, Nan. I do."

"All right. Go to her. I won't make any trouble."

Smiling, he said, "I'll still see you now and then. As often as I dare."

She shrugged, turned and left.

Picking up his saddlebags, Tremaine descended the stairs. His horse had been brought from the stable and was tied in front of the hotel. He lashed the bags to the cantle, mounted and turned south, a long ride ahead that could be shortened somewhat if he went by way of the desert. But the Indians made that extremely dangerous for a man traveling alone. He would go through Yreka, the closest telegraph office, and wire Lorna that he had just heard of her arrival and was on his way. Then he could cut across the mountains by way of Noble's Pass and Honey Lake.

He thought that he had handled Nan very well, and now that the break had been forced on him he was relieved to have it over. Yet the freeing brought with it a sense of guilt of mixed origins. Nan couldn't hold a candle to Lorna in beauty, personality or character, and his lack of taste in the matter troubled him more than a feeling of responsibility. He would not have got so involved with Nan, he thought, except for the disinterest she had shown in him during their early acquaintance. She had a streak of cynical honesty that often made her blunt and irritating. She had turned his blandishments aside impatiently, and the night he first kissed her she had remained unstirred until, on fire with frustration, he had handled her so roughly she had at last responded. After that she had been a woman in love, like any other.

He bypassed Jacksonville, staying on the older emigrant road that followed Bear Creek through the hamlet of Central Point and pressing on through Phoenix. By the time he reached the upper valley he had begun to discern that Lorna's willful disregard of his objections could have been a disguised blessing. Any time now, the West would be under a different government. It would be awkward, even crippling to him, to be too involved with Nan after that had taken place.

Once he was powerful, perhaps the leading figure on the coast, she would be all the more reluctant to give him up to another woman, a woman much better suited to share his role. And Lorna had to know eventually what his purpose out here was. She had to be won around, loyal little Ohioan that she was — and as he had once been. She had to see the hopelessness, the injustice of the Union cause, the inevitability of defeat, and his wisdom in choosing the side that would leave him strong, a far more important man than he could ever have been otherwise.

He had never doubted the outcome of the struggle in which the nation was locked. The pacifist spirit was still strong in the North, crippling Lincoln. The War Department and Army of the Potomac, on which the defense of the east rested, was shot through with indecision and lethargy. The Army had been routed twice under aging Scott, and McClellan, the new commanding general, showed no more eagerness for aggressive warfare. Washington could be taken any time the South considered it desirable. If that did not break the will of the North completely, the shattering loss of the West would. Since he would have played an important role in delivering the West, he could emerge openly, a great hero to much of the nation rather than the traitor he would be branded if he were caught prematurely.

He stopped for a meal at Cole's Station, and by late afternoon had topped the twisting Siskiyou grade and dropped down to the Klamath crossing. The ferry took him immediately over, and he was soon following up the Shasta Valley, passing Hawkinsville, then coming to Yreka, his destination for that day. The brisk cold of the high country had chilled him, and as he rode into the town he could see Mount Shasta rear white and icy into the heavens on south. He saw also that a Hackett pack-string was in the corral on the edge of town and wondered if Hack was with it. He hoped so. He had had no report from the man in several weeks.

He rode on to the telegraph office, which was the end of a spur line coming up from the overland system. He took pains with the telegram he filed for Lorna, addressed to the International in Virginia City, explaining his failure to meet her, informing her he would be there in two days more, assuring her of his eagerness to see her and of his complete love and devotion. He paid the charge and, feeling that he had righted his private world, returned to the street.

Yreka rivaled Jacksonville as the metropolis of the border country, having sprung to life as a gold camp a decade before, later acquiring added importance as the trading center for an agricultural and stock raising area, always an important waypoint on the busy road between Oregon and California. He left his worn horse at a livery barn and, carrying the saddlebags, tramped on to the hotel he regularly used when here. He was tired and stiff from the long ride, yet a lively energy stirred him. He had missed Lorna more than he had let himself acknowledge. It was so like her spunky little spirit to defy him, and now that he had evaluated the situation carefully, he was pleased that she had done so.

He washed up, combed his hair, and went down to the bar for a drink before having his supper. He had never based here, but had been through enough times to see several men he knew in a casual fashion. He exchanged a word with each of them, always affable, although none were important to him and his plans. The high country would fall automatically once he had encircled it, and the fewer who knew the plan, the better.

He ate alone, bought a handful of cigars at the desk and lighted one, then went out to the street. He walked slowly, idly, as if only taking the saddle kinks out of his muscles, but he made a point of passing the corral where he had seen mules with the Hackett brand. Hack still was not there, but one of his helpers was and said the man was in camp. Tremaine left word for him to come to his hotel room and returned to it, himself.

It was nearly an hour before a knock sounded on his door. At his call, Hackett came in, bewhiskered and grimy and with his usual swaggering walk. Tremaine rose, smiled and offered his hand, although he both despised and admired his hireling, liking his cynical opportunism, his aggressive, often brutal courage, yet repelled by his coarseness, his taste for cheap booze, brawling, and brief contacts with easy women.

Hackett said cheerfully, "You see the bulletin?" and, when Tremaine shook his head, added, "Just come over the wire, and they tacked it outside the newspaper office. They've found out that Sibley's at Fort Bliss, with twenty-three hundred men gathered there. It's scared the pants off a good half of this town. They see him barrelin' right over the desert and taking this country."

"The officials know what he's up to," Tremaine said easily. "And there isn't a thing they can do."

"Dunno," Hackett said with a shake of the head. "Can't jump off for a couple of months yet. They might come up with something to stop him."

"What with? A handful of untrained militia? Sibley'd slice right through them. What have you been up to, Hack? I expected to see you before now."

"I can talk to you any time," Hackett returned, with his typical insolence, "and I've got a lot to do before snow flies and shut down the trails. For one thing, I brought the last of the stuff in from Eureka, right from under the nose of the Army at Fort Humboldt. Say, did you know U. S. Grant was stationed at that fort just five or six years ago? That jigger who's trying to hold back the Rebs on the Mississippi?"

"I neither knew nor care," Tremaine said. "Come over the mountains?"

Hackett shook his head. "Up Little River and then the Trinity. Nobody looked at us twice. Why should they? The stuff was packed in sand in sugar sacks. The way we run the rest. It's safe on the Yuba, and I'm on my way home to J'Ville, thank God."

"Good. Have any trouble taking the stuff over to Groot?"

Hackett's face sobered. "No, but I've got something to tell you we didn't figure we should trust to the mail. And it wasn't worth making a special trip to see you. It might not mean anything."

"Oh?" Tremaine said and frowned.

"You remember that key pounder who's

crazy about a little gal I know in Virginia City? She leads him on because I told her to for what she can worm out of him. Well, he picked up some business the Army was sending over the wire, not even in code. About a undercover man bein' sent out here from Jefferson. Or that's the way it sounded."

"Give his name?"

"They weren't that stupid. But Fort Churchill was to furnish him with a list of suspects. So Groot bribed a stock tender at Churchill station to watch for an exchange between a stage passenger and somebody from the fort. A little later this fella come pounding in with word it had happened. From the description, the boys figured it was a bird named Dalton who registered at the International."

"Dalton?" Tremaine said sharply. "You sure?"

"Yeah. You know him?"

"Saw him yesterday evening in Gold Hill. He was the one who told me my wife's in Virginia City, and why I'm on my way there. My God."

Hackett opened his mouth and rubbed his jaw. "Me, too. We decided the boys had pegged the wrong man."

"Why?"

"Well, Groot set a man to tailing Dalton. That Joe Sanders, if you remember him. Dalton obliged by taking a walk over the divide. Sanders jumped him and got himself killed."

"Jumped him? What for?"

"Groot wanted to see that list and find out who the Army figures is responsible for those army guns they found on the Humboldt. Wouldn't you?"

"Yes," Tremaine admitted, "but that was a reckless move, and I'll tell Groot so when I see him."

"He covered it, I think. This Dalton come out to the Silverhorn the next morning I happened to be there. He come right out and said Sanders had demanded a list. He figured the lunkhead was off his rocker. With Dalton talkin' that way, we decided the boys had let the real army man slip through their fingers."

"Maybe they did," Tremaine said hopefully. "Dalton's pretty well connected. He knows Henry Klippel. He's been looking around for a mining prospect to invest in. But damn Groot for tying it to us, because it could be Dalton."

"Spilled milk now. We just won't let anybody we ain't sure of in on anything. And watch Dalton so if he starts gettin' hot we can do something about him. Anyhow, there's two parts to his puzzle. He can get a long ways with one, but till he's got both he can't do us any damage."

"That's right," Tremaine agreed. "Well, it's the imponderables of fate, I guess."

Hackett laughed. "How you do like fancy words. So your wife's come to join you, finally. How's Nan goin' to like it when she finds out?"

"She knows, and she doesn't like it."

"Too bad. She's a nice kid. I doubt you'd have made so much time, Tremaine, if she'd known you're already teamed up."

"You're hardly the man to get moral," Tremaine was amused. "But never mind. Will you do me a favor? As soon as you reach Jacksonville, rent a house for me. Furnished. Offer enough rental to get a good one, even if the present occupants have to move to other quarters."

"You mean you're bringing the missus to J'Ville?"

"Why shouldn't I?"

"No reason, if that's how you want it. But I wouldn't bet on which woman'll blow off the roof." Hackett turned toward the door, and there paused to glance back. "About Dalton. If he's the army man, he ain't in touch with 'em regular. If he just disappeared, they might not find out about it till we've already picked out posies."

Tremaine shot him a sharp glance, then found the idea appealing. "That's right. Unless he's taken local people into his confidence. We'll see."

He undressed leisurely after Hackett had left, reflecting on how much he owed Hackett and Nan and a few men like Oscar Groot. Nan had been in southern Oregon a number of years and had steered him on to men in key positions, not zealots or Southern patriots but simply men who could be corrupted. They in turn were working among the high principled ones, people who sincerely thought the West should tie its destiny to the Confederacy, in whose cause they believed. Tremaine had a vast contempt for this latter class, but he would use them readily.

Hackett had recruited the cadres now passing as mine crews, reckless, rapacious men equal to anything that would profit them personally. And he had promised them much. Groot and men like him had served in the way Nan had, on the Comstock, the Yuba and Illinois. None of these had one grain of principle, let alone patriotic dedication to the South. Yet somehow they were the ones with whom he felt the most at ease.

He was off at daybreak and on the second evening rode up the long Geiger grade into Virginia City. He left his horse at a livery and, since Lorna would be using the quarters he had not yet relinquished here, he went to a barbershop for a bath and shave. The supper hour had arrived by the time he walked into the International lobby.

The desk clerk gave him a warm and unctuous greeting. "Welcome back, Mr. Tremaine! And perhaps we have a delightful surprise for you!"

"No, I heard, although belatedly. Do you know if my wife's come down for supper?"

"I hardly think so, sir. One — uh, notices a lady as stunning as Mrs. Tremaine."

Tremaine ascended the stairs two at a time. He knew Lorna had received his wire when the door flew open at his first rap. "Alan!" she cried. "Oh, Alan!"

"Lorna, darling!"

He half carried her into the sitting room and kicked the door shut with his foot. Her hungry kisses made him wonder why he had even found another woman interesting. He returned them with the kind of aggressive tenderness he knew she liked to have from him.

Finally she murmured, "I thought you'd be too angry to speak to me, even."

He loosened her, and they moved apart. Laughing, he said, "Now that you've done it, I'm glad. Maybe I was reluctant to take the responsibility if you're miserable out here. Now it will be your own fault if you are."

"What kind of fragile flower do you think I am?"

"Where we're going to live won't be like this. I've got to move my headquarters to a location more central to my interests. We'll be in Jacksonville."

"As long as we're together, who cares where it is?"

"It's not exactly primitive," he assured her. "I've asked a friend to rent us a nice furnished house."

"A house? Oh, Alan, it will be so glorious to have a home again. When do we start?"

"Now that I'm here, I might as well attend to some business. Day after tomorrow, perhaps. I came across the mountains horseback. That's much too rough for you. We'll take the stage by way of Sacramento."

"I'm sick to death of stages," she retorted, "and you know very well I'm as good a rider as you are. We'll go the way you came."

"Very well," he laughed. "I should know by now that you have the stubbornness of a Missouri mule. But I love you for it."

Chapter 8

The fat flakes drifted down in feathery softness. Each seemed to live, Tracy thought, for only the second in which it dropped through the lamplight beyond the window. There was no wind, and if there was movement in the street outside the saloon, its sound was muffled by the snow. The outdoor stillness seemed to sharpen the clink of chips behind him, the murmur of voices, the scrape of chairs. The storm had caught the northbound stage out of Waldo. By the time it reached Kerbyville the road was four inches buried. So the driver had declared a layover until morning and dumped his seven passengers on the porch of the big frame hotel.

Tracy pulled on his cigar, its glow reflecting in the window through which he idly watched. Had he received Klippel's message a few days earlier, he could have got back to Jacksonville ahead of the storm. The letter had been cryptic, saying, "If you haven't got onto something to hold you there, I suggest you return the earliest possible. A prospect worth looking into has turned up here." He had known this was Klippel's way of saying Abe Jewett had accomplished what they had asked of him. Tracy could have his secret look into Tremaine's suspected mine, as soon as he could reach Gold Hill.

He had been in the west section of Southern Oregon for two weeks, and it was now mid-December. He had acquainted himself unobtrusively with Tremaine's Gold Star, in one of the gulches out of Waldo. Its crew, Tracy had determined, was the same kind of hard-faced men he had found around Tremaine's other mines. At Klippel's suggestion, he had talked with Chance McCabe, the local sheriff, and taken him into his confidence. McCabe seemed competent, and had fought in the early Indian wars. Tracy knew that if the rebellion did come off, this section would not be caught napping. That was all he had hoped to achieve, while waiting for the way to be prepared for him to inspect the Lady Luck, in Gold Hill, in stealth.

"It don't look like we'll even get out in the morning," a fretting voice said at Tracy's elbow. He turned to see a drygoods drummer who had been on the stage. He was a fleshy man, and his cheeks had turned red in the heat of the saloon, where most of the stranded travelers had come to kill the long evening.

Tracy said, "Well, it's a bad town."

The drummer shook his head. "I've just got to connect with the stage to Portland. The family's looking for me home for Christmas."

"That's a week off yet. You'll make it."

A laugh erupted from a bearded prospector who sat nearby. He had seemed asleep, but now admitted to eavesdropping. "Gents," he drawled, "don't be surprised if you spend your Christmas right here. Ten years ago a storm started like this that cut us off from everything for months. Real gentle like, it was. No wind, all soft and purty. Trouble was, it just never stopped long enough for a man to stick his nose outdoors, even."

Suspiciously, the drummer said, "You trying to rib me?"

"Nope. It's just the way this thing's startin' out. That winter —"

Tracy realized the old gasser had only tried to arrest attention so he could start unwinding his tales. The camps were full of his type, leatherly old codgers who had come in with the first placer rush and stayed on after the bars played out, prospecting and doing well enough to keep in bacon and beans. They lived mainly for the evenings or stormbound days when they could collect somewhere and regale each other, but preferably credulous strangers, with their tales.

The drummer, understandably, was interested in what was to come, but Tracy was not. Pulling his coat tighter together, he stepped into the street. Kerbyville was newer than most of the western camps, but it had become the largest town in the valley of Illinois. Yet all Tracy could see was a hint of lamplight at intervals along the street. The frozen fluffs of snow stroked his face, and the pack rustled and crunched under his boots while he made his way back to the hotel.

He undressed as soon as he reached his room, for it was none too warm. But the blankets were thick, and once he was in bed he relaxed in drowsy comfort. At such times a man's thoughts strayed to pleasant things, and he wondered about Lorna Tremaine. It was hard to pick a feature he would call her best: her eyes and their sensitivity, her divine body, her quick gaiety and temper and her wonderful willfulness.

By now Tremaine would have joined her, and Tracy wondered how the man would handle the situation she had created so stubbornly. For that matter, it was time he considered the situation he would himself create for Lorna by doing nothing more than his duty required. Tremaine was as guilty of treason as he was of infidelity. There was room to hope that Lorna knew no more of the first, or would any more condone it, than she did the second. Tremaine's unmaking would bring him far more than disillusionment. In time of war, treason carried the penalty of death.

Tracy had expected to lie late abed and was surprised when a rap sounded heavily on his door before daylight. A voice called, "Stage's goin' out. Breakfast's on the table. Rise and shine."

He answered with sleepy gruffness and swung out of bed into the chilly air. Before he lighted the lamp, he walked to the window and looked out. A bright moon hung over a frozen landscape, and he was surprised to see that it had completely stopped snowing. Finding a match, he touched flame to the lamp wick and dressed quickly. The other passengers had been aroused and were in the lobby or dining room. The stocky drummer was beaming, bound to reach home in time to help fill his children's Christmas stockings. Tracy clapped him on the shoulder, grinning.

"So the old codger was wrong, this time," he said.

The drummer laughed. "You must've gone to bed early. It had quit by the time I could get away from him."

Neither driver nor horses were strangers to snow country, and the stage rolled steadily. By the time it reached the Applegate, where the fall had been lighter, it was making good time. On the following evening, Tracy re-registered at the Robinson House in Jacksonville.

He had learned Klippel's local address at the desk, and it was the clerk's opinion that the man was in town, for he had seen him on the street that day. So Tracy cleaned up and changed clothes, planning to drop over to Klippel's house later in the evening, after the supper hour. That left him with a couple of hours to kill, and even after a leisured meal there was an hour to go. He stepped out to California Street.

There had only been a couple of inches of snow here, and the walk had been shoveled off. He tramped along the street and all at once stopped in pleased surprise. He was passing Bruner's mercantile, and Lorna Tremaine came through its door toward him. She carried a small package in her hand and was alone. She started to pass by, then stopped.

"Tracy Dalton! Why — hello again!"

"Welcome to Jacksonville."

"I understand you'd left."

"And returned. I like this place. Even better than I thought. Are you paying us a visit?"

"We've rented a house," she said happily. "I'm here to stay."

"Wonderful."

"You must drop in and see us. Alan said he'd met you. We're on C Street, between Fourth and Fifth. The house on the south side, behind a hedge."

"I'll surely be there, but I've got to go to Gold Hill in the morning. I might not be back right away."

"What's wrong with this evening? Alan's home."

Ruefully, Tracy said, "Gosh, I've got to do something else this evening. If I dared, I'd surely put it off."

"Later, then."

"You can lay a bet on it."

Lorna smiled and went on, and Tracy marvelled that this warm, diffusing pleasure should come to him at the mere sight of another man's wife. Of a mortal enemy's wife, he reminded himself. Yet he meant to see her, if Tremaine would stand for it. He had his own stake in Lorna's welfare, which he probably took a lot more seriously than did her husband.

Henry Klippel answered his door, an hour later, and said jovially, "Heard the stage got through finally and hoped you were on it. Come in. Betty — that's the wife — went to a woman's doings at the church. Old Abe come through, and he's as anxious as I am to see what good it'll do."

Grinning, Tracy said, "That's what I thought you meant." The room was bright, cheerful and well furnished for a frontier home. A big, polished heater gave off a glowing warmth, and Klippel motioned him into a cushioned rocker, then offered a box of cigars. They lighted up, Klippel returning to a Morris chair. "When do I go in?" Tracy added.

"What's wrong with tomorrow night? Near as I can tell, Tremaine's outfit is aboveground then. Abe and me figured to let it get around that he's got something pretty hot in the Yellow Jacket, that he's thinking of taking you on as a partner. If you find something in the Lady and want to stick around, that's a good excuse. If not, you can say you decided against it."

"A good suggestion."

Klippel pulled on his cigar. "What did you learn over west?"

"Nothing I could move in on. But I figure the Lady'll tell the story for the other mines. What I find there will go for all. I posted McAbe. He'll be set to seize the Gold Star the minute he gets word from us to do so."

His host nodded. "Good. I had a talk with Johnny Ross. Being an officer, himself, he took the trouble to check on you. Bart Traxler's answer convinced John, and he wants to help you. It'll be easy to see him. He owns a piece of the Gold Hill. I can arrange for you to bump into each other there."

"Thanks. Captain Traxler didn't exaggerate the help I'd get up here."

"It's our country, damn it. With you, an outsider, running the big risks. Makes me want to kick myself, when I think how easy we were to take in."

"Long ways from the war out here," Tracy offered. "It doesn't hit home like it does with people closer to it."

"Besides, people who come out to spend the rest of their lives feel they're coming to a brand new country. Usually something's caused 'em to turn their backs on the East. Hard times, the crowdedness, the ague in the Central States. And this is a land of promise. It don't belong to anybody but them." Klippel leaned forward to tap cigar ash into the draft of the heater. "Want to buy a good saddlehorse?"

"I was going to ask where I could."

"Figured you'd want one. Man likes his own animal, and he can board one cheaper than rent if he gets around much. Reason I asked is Charlie Dunsing brought some fine fellas over from his ranch on Bear Creek. Anything he raises and gentles is fit to throw leather on. They're at the Arkansas and for sale."

"I'll have a look."

"Walk over with you, if you like. Wouldn't mind a drink, and I don't keep it in the house."

An hour later, Tracy had a bill of sale for a strong-bottomed bay that sold itself to him in one short ride out the stage road and back to the livery. He bought a secondhand saddle and bridle at the stable, then took Klippel over to the Howling Wilderness and stood the drinks. The surroundings reminded him of Ridge Durnbo, and he asked about him.

"Ridge?" Klippel said. "Sure. He's a heller, but he's sound as a new dollar."

"Could I trust him?"

"No doubt about it."

"Well, I've wondered if he might have seen something out along the emigrant road, last summer, that would suggest something about how the smuggling was done. If I find the stuff in the Lady, of course, that part's over. If I don't, I might want to talk with Durnbo."

"By the way," Klippel said, and lowered his voice. "I run into Tremaine the other day. He felt me out about you. I built you up as a mining man I've known from way back. Seemed to ease him."

Then Klippel said his wife was due home from her church meeting, and he had best get back. Since the man had become his open sponsor, they agreed to ride out to Gold Hill together the following morning.

The day dawned clear and crisp, the horses were strong and fast, and shortly after ten o'clock Klippel and Tracy reached the Yellow Jacket mine. Abe Jewett was on the surface, impatiently awaiting their arrival. He had fired up the pot-bellied stove in the little shack that served as his office, warehouse and sometimes living quarters. He was a gaunt man, stooped and bald, and his rangy frame had the tough look of leather. He smoked a pipe of potent odor.

"So you're the ring-tailed snorter," he

commented, "that aims to skin some polecats."

"With your help, Mr. Jewett, I hope to."

"Abe, for criminy sakes. You'll get all the help I can give you. I got four sons in the war. Matt, Mark, Luke and John. That's as far as me and the missus got through the Good Book, afore I lost her. Klip tell you what we done?"

Klippel shook his head. "Left that to you, Abe, since you did the work."

Abe cackled. "By damn, Tracy, we jabbed the Lady right in the seat of her pants. Once old Klip persuaded me he weren't batty, I got ambitious, myself, for a look in that mine. It's a pocket mine — everything on this hill is, includin' Klip's hole in the ground. What money me and the boys took out of the Lady was early. The pocket played out, and that's all there was in that drift. We cut more and dropped down a couple of levels, but on them we hardly made expenses. Get what I'm drivin' at?"

"Well," Tracy said, "I didn't figure Tremaine's making money or expects to."

"That's right. I figured that old pocket's where he'd store anything he wanted to hide in the mine. Lots of room, and it's in an out of the way part. Been no work in that area in a couple of years."

"The Lady's hind pocket," Tracy said. "Where you jabbed her."

"That's it. I knew where that pocket was and had a drift here in the Yellow Jacket that comes within a hundred feet of its back wall. It didn't matter if we run a mite high or low or right or left, we had a big target. So we went on it. Inside of a week we holed through. I couldn't have figured it better if I could have used a transit."

"Wonderful," Tracy breathed. "What did you find in the pocket?"

"That's where the story ain't so good," Abe said. "Nothin'."

"So?"

"We didn't go any farther. Klip had said not to, ourselves. But there's your entrance, and they ain't apt to find it. I don't think any of them's been in that old gallery since they took over. We holed through with a coyote small enough to cover with old timbers on their side."

"Good," Tracy said. "We couldn't expect it to fall in our laps."

Klippel looked at his watch and said, "I'd better get to work, Tracy. I'd say you'd best stay here till night, like you were looking over Abe's property and talking business. Safer than trying to sneak back after dark, tonight. Abe lives out here a lot of the time, anyhow."

"Got a house in town," Abe explained, "but it can sure get lonesome with my boys off to war."

Klippel said he would have John Ross come to his mine the next morning and left. Tracy carried his saddlebags into the shack, then he and Abe put the horse in the shed where the old man kept the mule that worked in the arrasta. Afterward they stepped into the mine tunnel, where Abe lighted lanterns. He loved his mine and took pride in showing it, although it was making him no fortune. His men knew what Tracy was there for but made no reference to it. His snap judgment was that they were trustworthy.

It didn't take long to explore the working faces, then Abe took Tracy into a freshly cut drift that, at its end, tapered to a coyote hole through which a man would have to crawl on his belly. They didn't talk because its sound could carry dangerously into the other mine, but the gleam in the old man's eyes said enough. Tracy clapped him on the shoulder, and they went back to the shack, where Abe cooked a delayed noon meal.

"Don't suppose you'd let a man go in the Lady with you," Abe said hopefully.

Tracy grinned but shook his head. "Rather not, Abe. Not that I wouldn't be glad of your company. But I want a man who knows where I am if I'm not back after a reasonable time. That'll be you."

"I guess you're right," Abe said reluctantly.

They ate. Abe had work to do, but they were supposed to be talking business, in case somebody was keeping tabs. So he spent the entire afternoon in the shack with Tracy, regaling him with tales of his experiences in and out of almost every mining camp in the Far West. Twice he had become a rich man, only to go broke with equal speed. At five o'clock it was growing dark. At six the crew knocked off, the men going down the canyon to homes in the town. Abe cooked another meal. He was a good cook and believed in eating well. Afterward Tracy reciprocated with a cigar, and they talked for another couple of hours.

In spite of himself, Tracy felt his nerves tighten. His fear was not so much from the danger of being caught out of bounds, although he did not discount that. He had gambled two weeks of precious time on this venture. Good men had gone to work and expense to help, and the coming hours could show he had made a very bad guess.

Chapter 9

At eight o'clock Abe lighted a lantern and struck down the road toward the Lady, his legs thrown long and black against the bank on the uphill side. He walked briskly, rounding the headland, and seeing far below him the dim clutter of lights of the village. Dark clouds were scrubbing the face of the moon, and he could hear the wind file against a thousand obstructions. When he came to the short turn-off to Tremaine's mine, he took it, observing that the handful of surface shacks showed light. The tunnel adit was dark, but he knew there was a gallery at the first vertical shaft, and that Tremaine kept a couple of men there through the night. The gallery was too far in for the light by which they played poker and swilled coffee to show outside. They were kept there to prevent anyone's penetrating to the vital part of the mine from the surface without their knowing it.

Abe cut a slant toward the oblong building that served as a bunk and mess house for Tremaine's oversized crew, taking comfort in the fact that business of one sort or other often brought him here at odd hours. The noise from within seemed normal. He opened the door and stepped in.

Several heads turned toward him, although most of the dozen men there paid no attention. Abe said, "Howdy, boys." He was glad they had never had any reason to distrust him.

They nodded, and Bide Tugwell, Tremaine's right bower, said, "What're you doin' out in the dark, Abe?"

"Tremaine around?"

"Was," Tugwell grunted. "But he went back to J'Ville this afternoon. Whatcha want of him?"

"Got a feller lookin' at the Jacket. Can't make him understand how the two mines lay together. There's a old drawing I turned over to Tremaine when he bought the Lady. Thought mebbe he'd lend it back a bit."

"You'd have to see him about that."

"Be out tomorrow?"

"Said he would. Who's the sucker?"

"Name's Dalton. Hails from Colorado, and he's got a piece of loose change."

"What you want to sell out for?"

"We're only dickerin' on an interest. I'm runnin' short of money."

Tugwell laughed. “Well, I hope you sucker him.”

Abe grinned back. “Like the sayin’. Let the buyer beware.”

Ten minutes later he was back at the Yellow Jacket, where Tracy awaited him.

“Don’t think they smell a thing,” Abe reported. “Tremaine’s in Jacksonville and wouldn’t be there if he figured somethin’ was up here. I dropped your name, and it caused nary a ripple.” He took a lantern off a wall peg and handed it to Tracy. “Don’t light it till you’re in a hundred feet or so. Just follow the car tracks. There’s nothin’ to trip you up.”

Nodding, Tracy said, “Don’t worry if I take a while.”

“If you ain’t back here at daybreak, I’m goin’ for the militia at Camp Baker.”

Tracy laughed, but he did not discount the hazards in his undertaking. Stepping out into the night, he walked swiftly to the tunnel mouth and vanished. The twin rails used by the ore cars guided him into an inky blackness. When presently he looked back, the adit had shrunk to the size of a postage stamp. He lighted the lantern and by its light quickly found the drift leading to the new coyote hole. He could feel the muscles tighten across his shoulders.

The drift carried him another hundred feet, at right angles in the main tunnel. He could tell by new shoring where Abe's outfit had begun the extension which, after about eighty feet, terminated in a partial wall. The last ten or fifteen feet required him to wriggle along like a snake, shoving the lantern ahead. Then he was confronted by old four-by-four timbers placed crosswise outside the hole. These were inside the old pocket of the Lady, and Tracy felt his pulse speed up.

Placing the lantern behind him, he began to move the timbers, working them to one side until he had a free end he could pull in and shove on behind him. That gave him room to work, and the rest of the pieces could be shoved aside in the pocket. In less than five minutes he was through and standing in a musty catacomb, deep in the gold-rich hill. He left the lantern where it was and rose to a stand, motionless for a moment to let his eyes adjust.

Presently he could see jagged walls that once had contained the main wealth of the Lady. Dust lay on the upper surfaces of rocks and across the floor. The walls drew in at some distance ahead of him, shrinking to a normal-sized drift. The pocket had never presented a hazard and had not been blocked off. But it was on the main mine level, Abe had told him, although it was canted at an angle to the tunnel and the other drifts that, after the first bonanza played out, had explored deeper into the mountain. A level fifty feet below had also been explored. A winze at the end of the upper level, Abe had said, would let him down to the lower.

He waited in darkness, feeling lonely and acutely conscious of the men kept through the night at the main shaft, between his present position and the adit on the surface. He must be at some distance from them, for he could hear nothing nor see a hint of light. He had a choice between carrying the lantern or risking an accidental, noisy collision with something. He picked light as his best bet. Returning, he got the lantern, turned it down to a minimum glow, then moved cautiously out toward the main tunnel.

The car tracks, where he came into the tunnel, showed they were being used. A pale speck of light showed at the end of the reach to his right. He turned away from it, proceeding in the other direction. The air grew warmer as he pressed deeper into the interior, following the tunnel still but investigating each side extension. He came to one such, presently, where work was being done, principally, he knew, to provide waste rock to push out to the dump to lend a legitimate look to the mine. Drills, striking hammers, shovels, picks and wheelbarrows cluttered the floor in that area. There was nothing of any special interest.

Tracy was sweating by the time he reached the winze, and the air had grown humid and stuffy. Dipping light into the dark well before him, he saw dust on the rungs of the ladder dropping down, proving it had long been in disuse. But he had to try his luck on the level below and, swinging over, he descended swiftly, nearly choking on the stirred dust. This was the end of the lower level, too, he discovered. Car tracks had been laid to it but were badly rusted. He could risk turning up the lantern now and did so, then moved ahead. He could hear water drip somewhere, and once a sudden racket under his feet nearly stopped his heart. Then he saw a rat scoot off ahead of him. He went on for nearly a hundred feet before he found a drift to the side. A flash with the light showed him it was caved in, with nothing suggestive visible between him and the tumbled debris.

Tremaine's crew didn't seem to be doing

anything on this level. The one stop above, apparently, supplied all the waste they needed to create the impression that the mine was being worked seriously. He walked steadily, figuring that the contraband he hoped to find was heavy enough to induce them to use an ore car to move it. The tracks he followed were still badly eroded with rust. And so it remained until, all at once, he saw a dim reflection of light ahead. He halted summarily and turned down his lantern. That was the main shaft, and the gallery where the guards spent their time was just above. He frowned. He had covered everything except the area close to them on the level above. It had been without result.

He stood stubbornly for a moment then blew the lantern completely out and set it down at his feet. Very carefully he moved forward, the light ahead growing stronger as he approached. He began to hear the ragged, indecipherable sound of voices. Beyond the shaft was a blob of vague shapes. He came up to the edge of the light falling from above him, trembling, breathing faster. He could not make out what the men up there were saying, but it was obvious there were at least two of them.

Taking his life in his hands, Tracy

ducked through the indirect light and pressed into the darkness beyond, only to grow more puzzled.

What had drawn him was nothing more than a considerable store of blasting powder in the small, corrugated tin drums in which it was packed and shipped. Yet it seemed strange that such stuff would be kept here, under the feet of men who spent their nights in the gallery over him. He had never known of a mine that did not keep its explosives outside, and at a safe distance. He dropped a hand to one of the tins on the top layer and pushed. It was heavy. Much heavier than it should be.

He had to know what they really contained.

He went on farther, on this side of the light, but within fifty feet came to the blank face of the drift's end. There was nothing here but the powder, or whatever was in the drums. Turning back, he stopped at the stack. After a moment's listening, he worked his fingers under a drum on top and hefted it. He could carry it, with effort. He swung it to his shoulder and again waited, his belly muscles tight. Then he moved slowly and deliberately through the light and into obscurity again.

He paused to catch a breath, although

the shortness came from excitement more than exertion. Then he moved on slowly, stopped to pick up the lantern and, without lighting it, went on. It would be risky examining what might prove to be blasting powder by the light of a lantern. He had to get his stolen burden out of the Lady if he could manage it.

After a while he chanced using the lantern, as long as the drum was still sealed, and made faster progress. Nor did it prove as difficult as he had expected getting up the winze ladder to the upper level. The contents of the tin were stable and the can balanced well on his shoulder. But when he was up, he was confronted with the need to move closer to the guards. There was no other way to get back to the pocket and the coyote hole that would let him get back to Abe's mine.

He paused to rest, mopping his sweaty, now mud-smeared face with his handkerchief. Then he went on, the light again appearing ahead, enlarging and growing stronger. Presently he stopped and blew out the lantern and rested for a moment more. He watched the far light with edgy intentness. But the men standing watch there, night after night, would hardly expect to find an enemy behind them. He moved on again, and fifteen minutes later had replaced the timbers that covered the coyote hole.

He had got something, but was it what he wanted?

Another ten minutes brought him to Abe's shack, outside the mine. The old man heard him and opened the door, painfully curious and considerably relieved. Tracy stepped through quickly, and Abe shut the door.

"Whatcha want with the giant powder?" Abe said, while Tracy lowered the drum to the floor.

"I don't think that's what it is," Tracy said. He walked to the water pail and drank thirstily, then wiped his face again. "Who but a lunatic would keep his explosives inside his mine?"

"You found that inside the Lady?"

"And a lot more like it. Got a pinch bar?"

"Sure have, and we'll see what it is."

The round lid pressed into the top of the drum was easy to pry out. They saw not the black granules of blasting powder but, at first, a layer of cotton wadding used for packing. When that was pulled out of the can, loose cartridges fell from it to the floor.

"Goddlemighty!" Abe gasped. "You hit the jackpot!"

Tracy shook his head. "Took a trick, but that's all. I didn't find any guns, and what good's ammunition without them?"

"You could've overlooked 'em."

"Maybe, but I covered every foot of that mine except for the gallery where Tremaine's men were. I doubt the guns would be there, where some outsider might see them, entering the mine on business. They'd be cased for easier handling, and that would make them harder to hide and easier to find. It's my guess that they didn't put all their eggs in one basket."

"And hid the guns somewhere else?"

"That's my hunch, so far."

When they had emptied the container, they had a considerable heap of rifle, carbine and pistol shells on the floor. "Courtesy," Tracy drawled, "of the Union Armory at St. Louis."

"The cotton's to keep 'em from rattlin'."

"And to keep the cans from being too heavy for a man to handle. Must have been fifty or sixty just like this, Abe. Probably there's a similar store in each of Tremaine's other mines. To supply the local insurgents, when the rebellion starts."

"We know guns was run into the

country, too. That's what put you people onto the plot."

"So where are they?"

"Like you say," Abe offered. "A rifle case'd be harder to disguise, so they'd have to be hid better. Like in a secret drift that they've blocked off."

"There was one caved in," Tracy remembered. "But they'd want them so they'd be easy to move fast."

"It wouldn't take a crew a hour to clear away a cave-in. You've treed your coon, so why don't I take my boys in tomorrow night? We know that mine. We'd spot any new work quick."

"I wish you could," Tracy said regretfully, "but it's too dangerous, and not only to you and your men. I don't want Tremaine to know that I've finally got substantial evidence. The mines can be seized any time, the ammunition with them. But we've got to make sure we get the guns as well. If they keep those, they can scare up more ammunition. They might even have other caches."

Glumly Abe said, "Guess you're right. And I reckon we better repack this stuff and hide it real good, ourselves."

They had soon hidden the eloquent evidence in the Yellow Jacket. By then it was after midnight, and they went to bed.

Tracy had breakfast with Abe the next morning, then said, with a grin, "Still willing to go partners with me, Abe? That is, in the public eye?"

"I'm in with you to the hair," Abe said.

"Fine. I need a reason to be here that doesn't tie me down. So you announce a partnership. But say I'm only interested in putting my money to work, without much taste for soiling my lily-white hands. That'll let me hang around, yet come and go."

"It's as good as done. What're you going to do next?"

"I've got to go over and see Klippel. He said he'd have Ross at his mine, this morning. I don't know where I'll be after that, so don't expect me till you see me."

Tracy saddled the bay, an animal he had grown to like, and struck off down the road. The Lady Luck yard, when he passed, presented a picture of complete serenity. A man crossing to one of the buildings looked his way, but without particular interest. Klippel and Ross were down at the quartz mill, he learned at the Gold Hill mine. Tracy followed down the trail to the valley and found them there.

Ross proved to be older than Klippel

and himself, a man in his early fifties. He had grown portly and had a round, jovial face, and wore his wavy grey hair combed back. A thin goatee bisected his chin, but above the mouth was a fierce, full moustache. His eyes were genial, twinkling, and behind them was an unwavering light of will and courage.

"Quite a shock you brought us, Lieutenant," Ross commented, when they were closeted in the mill office. "Are you going to add to it, this morning?"

"Not a great deal, Colonel," Tracy said ruefully. "I found ammunition in the Lady Luck. Undoubtedly a part of the armory loot. But not a gun." He went on to describe his experience in Tremaine's bogus mine. "I wouldn't swear that I've gained much. At the first alarm, they'll move the stuff out. Maybe in dribbles, right under our noses."

"It's a touchy situation," Ross agreed. "I got to know the Lady pretty well in Abe's day. You say you used the old winze. You left hand and foot marks in the dust."

"Yes, sir, and probably in other places. If its discovered, and they check it out, Abe's in trouble, and our birds have flown the coop. On the other hand, they think they've got the place protected. I didn't get the impression anybody pokes around in the old part of the mine. So we might get away with it."

"If they thought you were getting too warm through some other lead, they'd move that ammunition."

"They would," Tracy agreed. "That's another reason we can't barge in and make wholesale arrests and seizures."

"I agree. We've got to keep them as complacent as we can, yet be prepared to close in on a moment's notice. Henry tells me you've posted Chance McCabe, and he's ready to do so at Waldo on signal. I've made the same arrangement with our sheriff. I've also filled in the officers at Camp Baker, so the militia company will be ready on call."

"That's fine," Tracy said. "Captain Traxler's doing something about the Yuba basin. Fort Churchill can handle the Comstock, provided something doesn't slip and let the thing get out of hand."

"With banana skins all over the place," Klippel put in.

"And," Tracy agreed, "the vital part of the puzzle yet to be solved. This is how I think they worked it. Those faked powder shipments could come in more or less openly by ship. Hackett could pick it up at

Crescent City and distribute it to the mines without too much danger of detection. If too much powder seemed to be going to any one mine, the tins could be packed in sugar or meal or hundred-pound flour sacks. Tremaine seems to run boarding houses at each of his operations. Partly, I suppose, to keep his men together."

"Cased guns wouldn't be so easy to move," Ross reflected. "Not through Crescent City, anyhow. Stuff's got to be lightered in over the tidal flats. So they sent the guns over the emigrant trail from the Missouri." He pushed back his hat. "Just the same, guns and shells have got to get together to make either worth a hang."

"I'm going to have another look in the Lady," Tracy told him. "Abe can go with me because he might notice something I'd miss. If I don't find it next time, then it probably isn't even in Gold Hill."

"Maybe they cached it somewhere along the trail," Ross suggested.

"I've considered that. It would give us a hopeless area to search, but, on the other hand, it would be risky for them. Supposing the Indians found such a cache? There wouldn't be a gun left when Tremaine wants them."

"Unless they've left a pretty heavy guard with them."

"Can you suggest such a place?"

Ross smiled. "I can suggest a hundred. If that's the trick, the cache could be any place this side of where the Indians burned the wagons. Farther down the Humboldt. On the Black Rock Desert. In the lake country. The Cascades. Anywhere in the Bear Creek Valley. Those are general localities, Lieutenant, with dozens of good hiding places in each."

Tracy rose from his chair. "It was nice meeting you, sir. I won't see you again unless forced to, but I'm glad to have you handling the ends I can't."

"I wish you luck, Lieutenant." The colonel offered his hand. "And I'm afraid we'll all need a lot."

Chapter 10

Tracy stood at the window of his room in Nan Bollinger's hotel, holding back the curtain and looking down into the road below. His hope of faster action, after his discovery in the Lady Luck mine, had met a swift end from an unexpected source. During the next night, the winter's second storm had rolled over the country, this one of blizzard intensity. For four days Tracy had been cooped up at the hotel while a shrill, knife-edged wind whipped snow like fine sand across the valleys and over the hills. It had let up yesterday, and once more things were on the move, for the northbound stage had just pulled up at the hotel porch. It had come from Jacksonville, and if it could get through, he could, also.

Hoping the wearing wait was over, he had yesterday visited the mercantile, across the road, to buy himself some heavy underwear, wool shirt and pants, a sheepskin coat and fur-lined gloves. Now he turned from the window and went to the bed to fish his saddlebags from under it. Into these he put a change of clothes and his toilet gear. Then, changed to the new, heavy clothes, he balanced the bags on his shoulder, left the room and descended the stairs.

The stage had made its team change and gone on. But Nan was still at the lobby desk, and she turned when she heard a tread creak under his weight. She was frowning slightly when he walked across to her.

"You're not leaving us?"

Tracy shook his head. "Only for a night or two. Looks like the road's open to Jacksonville."

"Hungry for the fleshpots?"

"Just for motion."

Beyond that, he reflected, he wanted news of the war. With stage service restored, the *Sentinel* would have received fresh dispatches from the wirehead at Yreka.

"Well, that's a livelier place to spend Christmas than here," Nan was saying.

"Christmas?"

"It's tomorrow. Didn't you know?"

He grinned. "I'm sorry. I have no family, and I guess I don't keep track of it."

"I have no family, either. But I still keep track of it."

"Well, Merry Christmas, then."

"The same to you."

Tracy was soon riding south along the rudely broken trail, aware that he had a long, slow ride ahead. Yet it seemed worth while, and he admitted that change and fresh news was the least part of his motive. He wanted to see Lorna. A week had passed since she invited him to call, and he hadn't even been back in Jacksonville. Tremaine had been caught on that end and would be home, so Tracy decided to drop in on them. The man might drop something helpful, and if he didn't, seeing Lorna would be reward enough.

The night after his discovery of the disguised ammunition, Tracy had paid the Lady Luck another visit, and Abe Jewett along to help. Inch by inch they had covered the ground he had searched by himself, only to be convinced that the guns were not in the mine. As Abe had put it, that had set them back to taw, or nearly.

The ride took him five hours, and it was four o'clock when Tracy left the bay at the Arkansas Livery. He got a room at the Robinson House, again, and changed to lighter clothing, then descended and ate an early supper for he had missed eating at noon. The establishment, like the town, had a warm, festive spirit that began to infect him. There was a Christmas tree in the lobby, decorated with tinsel, paper bells, popcorn strings and wax candles. Men he didn't even know invited him to join them at the bar.

Tracy pondered the propriety of giving a present to a married woman, then went up for his hat and sheepskin and stepped out to a street grown colder with the approach of night. The confectioner's, he remembered, was two blocks down from the hotel. There he purchased not one but two boxed assortments of French candies. Returning with these to the hotel room, he sat down to kill another hour by smoking a cigar.

It was nearly eight when finally he tramped out and found the house with the hedge. He wasn't sure what he would say to Tremaine, if he came to the door, but it was Lorna who answered his knock.

"Tracy Dalton!" she said, openly pleased. "I decided you'd left the country again."

"In this?" he said, laughing. "I've been playing solitaire in the Gold Hill hotel for the last four days."

"Do come in, and what a pity Alan isn't here." Lorna's features darkened. "The storm held up an important trip he had to make somewhere. He left early this morning. But he thought he'd get back sometime late tomorrow."

"And salvage part of Christmas," Tracy said, not bothering to conceal his disgust. "Well, here's something for the early stages of it, anyway." He handed her the box of candy he had brought with him from the hotel.

Lorna was surprised and pleased and opened the package while he hung his coat with his hat. "How nice!" she exclaimed. "And how thoughtful. Thank you. Won't you try them?"

"Mind if I have a cigar instead?"

"I'm not one of those fussy females who complain of their smell in the house. I like it. Let's sit by the fire."

They stepped from the hallway into a spacious and well-furnished parlor where a blaze filled the mow of a huge fireplace. Tremaine had at least provided his wife with attractive quarters. A stirring feeling of pleasure slid through Tracy, and he decided to steal brazenly the sharing of her Christmas Eve, which Tremaine had abandoned in the interest of his secret ambition. Lorna took a white-glazed cream from the box and placed the rest on the center table. She motioned him to a chair. Then she sat down across the fire from it, nibbling the candy, and he seated himself.

"How do you like Jacksonville?" he asked, and reached a cigar from his pocket.

"A charming place to live. I'm not well acquainted yet, but the people I've met are very nice." She smiled. "I fear I'm a little out of place with the women here. Most of them have children. I don't seem to get started along that line."

It bothered Tracy to think of her giving Tremaine a child. It would still have bothered him if the man weren't headed for disaster, if Tracy Dalton could manage to bring him to that end. Yet it was something Lorna longed for, undoubtedly, just as she had wanted, and finally had insisted on spiritedly, to make a home with the footloose man. Tracy had never had proof that she wasn't in on the plot, as he had first suspected, but somehow he didn't need it. This open, normal, wonderful young woman harbored no hunger for power, position, money, or whatever made an obvious native of the North swing his allegiance to the South.

"Tell me what you've been doing," she said.

"Well, I've bought an interest in the

Yellow Jacket at Gold Hill. Possibly you haven't got acquainted out there yet. It's next door to the Lady Luck, your husband's mine."

"Wonderful. You think it has possibilities?"

"Which mine?"

"Oh, Alan's sure he has a good thing."

"I'm sure of it, too," Tracy said dryly. He meant in Lorna. Watching her, the luster of her eyes in the firelight, the fresh, sensitive face, he wondered why Tremaine had lacked the sense to realize that, himself. Tracy looked about, adding, "You have a pleasant house."

"I love it. I'm trying to persuade Alan to buy it. But he thinks we'll only be here till he gets the mines organized. Then he says San Francisco or Sacramento would be better."

As the Confederate capital of the West, Tracy surmised. Aloud he said, "I bet you're a good cook."

"I certainly am."

"Well?"

She laughed. "I was about to invite you to supper, even without the flattery."

"Your husband and I aren't well acquainted. Would he mind?"

"Alan?" She looked surprised. "He's

glad I had you to help me when I found myself stranded in Virginia City. He'd like to know you better, I'm sure."

"Invitation accepted, then. But I've got to go back to Gold Hill tomorrow and might not be here again for a while."

"No notice required."

He began to draw her out about her background, which interested him. She was born in New York State, she said, but her parents moved to Cincinnati when she was quite young, and it seemed like her real home. She had met Alan there. He had worked for a river transportation company that plied the Ohio and Mississippi clear down to New Orleans.

Where he made his connections, Tracy reflected.

They had been married but a short while when the war broke out, Lorna said, and Alan had got the opportunity to go west for the financial syndicate she knew so little about. That had puzzled her, she admitted, when all the other men had rushed into the volunteer companies forming all over Ohio. But she understood it better now. Alan had explained how important the steady production of mineral wealth was to the Union cause. It helped to pay for the war, and it called for courage and hardihood, the same as fighting.

She was equally curious about Tracy, and he gathered that he had occupied her thoughts more than once since they parted in Virginia City. He could only summarize his part with a vagueness that he knew puzzled her. He had had an uneventful childhood in Pennsylvania and lost his parents in a fire when he was ten. Afterward had come a few years with an aunt and uncle in Illinois, then east to a military academy to polish off his education. Then the West, the first place he had felt really at home. This was where he meant to stay, without too much concern over who won the war. He knew she would repeat this to Tremaine, and, with Klippel's sponsorship and his supposed interest in the Yellow Jacket, it might serve to keep the Southern apparatus off balance a while longer.

He left at nine o'clock, not wanting to go but knowing Lorna was young and pretty enough to be talked about if she entertained a man too late in her husband's absence. Not until he was walking back to California Street did he realize that his desire to see her had made him forget his hope of fresh war news. He walked by the newspaper office on his way to the hotel.

There were bulletins tacked on the outside wall, but it was much too dark to read them.

He returned after breakfast, the next morning, and brought himself up to date. What good news there was came from Grant, the unknown and once-retired West Pointer who had been given a brigadier's commission and command of Union forces in Missouri. Grant was firming his grip on that vital section of the Mississippi. But in the east McClellan still hung around Washington, seeming more interested in the social functions of the capitol and the privileges of his high rank than in making good use of the Army of the Potomac. So far nothing had come of his rumored expedition by sea to attack Richmond from the rear. Lincoln himself was said to be highly dissatisfied with the general's failure to come to grips with the enemy. It was disappointing reading. McClellan had been considered a ball of fire when he took command, and his installation had enheartened the nation.

Tracy had puzzled over where Tremaine had gone in the first break in the storm, a journey that required his being away overnight. It had not been Gold Hill, unless he reached there early, for Tracy had not met him on the trail. He was about ready to return there himself, so he went down to the livery barn.

He had grown acquainted with the help at the Arkansas, and when his horse was brought to him he said idly, "Is this where Alan Tremaine keeps his animal?"

The hostler nodded. "That is, when he's in town."

"Do you know where he went this morning?"

"Left yesterday morning. Headed east, someplace, on the stage road. Never said where."

"See him next trip or at Gold Hill, I guess." Tracy paid the board bill and left. Tremaine's direction meant he had gone out on the California trail, but he couldn't even cross the state line and get home by the time he had set. Nor could he have gone far on the emigrant road to the desert.

Tracy reached Gold Hill in midafternoon and entered the hotel to find the lobby deserted. Climbing the stairs, he turned back on the landing that ran between the stair-rail and wall to the corner suite Nan occupied. She came at his rap. He handed her the second box of French candies he had bought in Jacksonville.

"Merry Christmas, Nan."

"Why — !" Nan's mouth opened. Her surprise changed to wonder, and the look in her eyes told him he had guessed shrewdly. This was a very lonely day for her. "How very thoughtful, Tracy. Thank you very much."

"My pleasure."

He turned and started toward his own door, but Nan's voice came gently after him. "Tracy." He turned back, and she added, "How long since you've eaten?"

"Breakfast."

"My goodness. I'll get something for you."

"Please don't. You have your rules, and I don't want you to break them for me."

"Rules are for the public," she said. "You come with me."

She took him down to the hotel kitchen. Her two Chinese, cook and helper, were off work at that hour, and she fried him eggs and made fresh coffee and toast. She sat down with him to drink coffee while he ate. He wondered if it were Tremaine she missed. The man had avoided her religiously since Lorna's arrival. Perhaps it was somebody else. Or something else. He knew she wasn't going to explain.

He went up to his room, lighted a cigar, and sat down with a map of Jackson

County that he had got from Henry Klippel previously. He knew from experience that the best of horses could not cover over thirty miles on road as they all were just now. That fixed the outermost limit of Tremaine's puzzling trip, so important to him he had risked letting his wife spend her Christmas alone to make it. Tracy scaled thirty miles with a piece of string and drew a circle on the map, with Jacksonville its center. The result was less than informative but it fixed the area to be searched first for the contraband guns.

Speculating, Tracy began to wonder if Tremaine could have gone over the divide to Jackass Creek and entered the Applegate country. The booming Steamboat mining district was on the headwaters of that stream. Tremaine was not known to have interests there, but one of his local associates might have. That was a possibility Tracy had not considered. It would be a good place to start, and he decided to strike off for there in the morning.

But again he was to awaken in the night to hear wind shrieking beyond the walls and grow aware of an intense cold in the room. There was a sound against the window glass like wheat being poured on paper. He concluded in sleepy indifference that the storm had started up again, then abruptly opened his eyes. Resumed with a vengeance! The wind rattled the window-sash and howled on the building corners. It was sleet that had started peppering the window. He snuggled deeper into the blankets and covered his ears, knowing he was not apt to leave for Steamboat when he had planned.

The sleeting had changed to a gentle but heavy snowfall when he awakened again in muggy daylight. He lifted his watch from the stand beside the bed and saw that it was eight o'clock. Cold nipped him when he threw back the covers, got up and dressed hurriedly. The hotel's population of regulars had gathered in the lobby. Once more they were snowbound.

Frustration bit at Tracy, but there was nothing he could do. And so it was for the next four weeks, in which a record storm battered Southern Oregon and the great desert, even the Rockies and great plains. There were interruptions in which no snow fell, but ground-blizzards rolled on the killing wind, buried roads and trails and slaughtered livestock and some of the men who tried to care for the animals. In the occasional clearings, a few men managed to get about on Norwegian snowshoes, but no vehicles moved and few saddle horses.

Cooped up at Nan's or the saloon or tradeless store, Tracy wondered about Ridge Durnbo and his partner, out on the open desert with their herd of cattle. For days on end, neither he nor Abe — who was caught in the village — could make it to the mine. But there were compensations. The enemy was equally impotent, Tracy knew, and could not steal a march. And he got to know Nan a great deal better during that interminable period.

Finally she told him why she was alone on the frontier. That had not been her state when she started west, for the start had been made in the company of her husband and six-year-old son. Cholera had attacked their train on the Platte river. She had escaped it, but they had died.

Chapter 11

A warm and thirsty sponge, the Chinook in late January wiped away the snow, flooding the streams and making bogs of the flat and flooded fields. But within the week the great valley hummed with renewed enterprise, the stranded, isolated and merely hung-up getting on with their purposes. And on Wickwire Creek, in upper Bear Creek Valley, Hack Hackett vigorously and profanely lashed his outfit into action to restore a badly disrupted schedule on which a great deal depended.

While he had an office and wagonyard on the edge of Jacksonville, here was the ranch where Hackett rested, doctored or boarded the hundreds of pack animals he owned and used in his far-flung business. To it, finally, the string caught away from the ranch by the blizzard had at last returned. And now he was hurriedly making up new units, not only to get on with his legitimate transportation business to the border towns and mines from Eureka, Crescent City and Scottsburg. Even more pressing was his badly delayed responsibility to Alan Tremaine, which now lay foremost in his thoughts.

Hackett had not seen Tremaine since the latter visited the ranch at Christmas time, where Hackett had been caught by the first round of snow. Tremaine had worried about the storm worsening and had tried to rush him. Now Hackett himself felt the urgency, for the big try was getting close, and he had learned something that troubled his always suspicious mind. When he had his various outfits dispatched, he took the last empty string, with two picked men, and hit the muddy trail to Jacksonville.

Reaching town in early afternoon, he left the men and mules at the corral and rode on up to Tremaine's house. Lorna answered the door, the pretty little trick who had surprised everyone by showing up as Tremaine's wife. Hackett had only seen her a time or two, since Tremaine discouraged an open association with him. He noticed with mild pleasure that she was taken back by his towering hulk.

"Lookin' for the mister," he said. "He around?"

"Why, no. He's at the mine."

Hackett grinned at her then, trying to frighten her, now that he knew she was here by herself. Creases formed on her brow. He thought the door moved a little, like she wanted to slam it in his face. He eyed her boldly for a long moment.

"No matter," he said finally. "I had to go out that way, anyhow."

She closed the door even before he turned away.

He rode to Oregon Street and swung north, and three hours later was at the Lady Luck, above Gold Hill. Tremaine was there, boredly killing time but forced to pretend that he was actively running his mine.

"I thought you'd be on your way to the cache by now," Tremaine said angrily when Hackett stepped into his office.

Hackett lifted a placating hand. "Don't get your hackles up. This bird Dalton bothers me. We've got to do something about him."

Tremaine simmered down. "Something new?"

"Not exactly." Hackett pulled out his tobacco plug and bit off a corner. "But I think we ought to test him before I tackle the next step."

"How?"

"By setting a trap. He works for the Army and knows your mines are bogus, but he can't get into one to prove it. So he's huntin' for other sign."

"That's your guess."

"If I prove it, will you let me tend to him proper?"

Tremaine's eyes hardened. "Prove it, and I'll attend to him. What do you have in mind?"

"One of my strings was caught at Steamboat. My man says Dalton was up there as soon as he could get through after the Chinook. Don't know what headed him that way, but he was askin' questions. Trying to see if you had an interest in something there, or any friends around."

Hackett knew his boss was interested, finally.

"So," Hackett resumed, "I'm gonna head there with an empty string. He'll follow, if he knows I'm doing it, and it'd be worth my time."

"How'll he know you're doing it?"

"Through Nan. Her pretty neck's as far out as ours, almost, and she don't want it stretched with a rope. I'll tell her what I think Dalton is and get her to drop a hint about me. He'll bite. And when he does, I'll kill him."

Tremaine lighted a cigar and puffed on it a moment. He shook his head. "Not immediately, at least. If he does, you're right, and there's a lot of information I'd want to sweat out of him. If he does what you think and you get him, bring him here."

Hackett rode swiftly down the grade to Nan's hotel. She was at the desk and only glanced at him impersonally. He knew she neither liked nor trusted him. There was no one else in the lobby, so he walked up to her, saying, "Howdy, Nan. How about us goin' upstairs?"

"Look here —"

"Take it easy," he said, laughing. "I got a message from Tremaine. Figured we better go up to your room where nobody can listen."

She said stiffly, "Nobody's listening."

"But you better. This Dalton you've got livin' here. Know who he's working for?"

"Himself."

"Not any. He's under cover for the Army."

Nan made a dismissing motion. "Oh, get out."

"If you want him to nail your hide to the fence, that's the way to get it done."

She regarded him uneasily. "What makes you think that?"

"I think it, and you're gonna help me prove it. Or, if you'd rather, you can help prove he ain't a army man, and we can all quit worryin' about him. Including Tremaine. He knows I'm down here to see you."

She wasn't convinced, and she didn't like him and what he had charged, but she said, "What do you want me to do?"

"Let somethin' drop to Dalton. That I'm takin' a empty string to Steamboat. Leavin' in the morning from J'Ville. If he's what I think, he'll figure I'm gonna run somethin' he's interested in. Why else'd I be going up there empty? He'll try to catch me at it."

"I have no reason to discuss you with him. He'd be suspicious."

"You better find a reason, if you don't want to find yourself in trouble." Hackett turned and walked out. He knew that she could not feel safe until she had tested Dalton, herself. Swinging onto his horse, he rode back to Jacksonville.

He packed up Jackson Creek the next morning, the mules spanking along briskly with their empty saddles, following a fairly clear trail. Once over the hump, he came to the Jackass and went down its valley, passing scene after scene of bygone mining activity. By noon he and his outfit had passed the Little Applegate, whose valley was more populous than that of the main stem that came down through tangled mountains from high in the Siskiyous. Steamboat lay up the major stream, on Carberry Creek, almost on the California line and too far for one day's travel in winter. Hackett didn't expect to have to go that far, if Dalton took the bait the way he hoped.

Swinging off the trail at noon, he and his men put the animals on picket and built a fire to make coffee. His helpers were Elvie Elveck and Trink Casey, young, hard-bitten and reckless, men who had helped him enough in shady enterprises to lend full support to this.

Elveck batched coffee and set the black old pot on the fire, spat tobacco juice and grinned. "Bet you scared Nan's pantaloons off her when you told her she's got a government man lookin' over her shoulder, Hack."

"Only way Hack could get 'em off," Casey put in.

"Shut up," Hack said good-naturedly. He liked being regarded as a rough fellow, one the ladies recoiled from instinctively. As long, that was, as women who didn't bother to be ladies regarded him more appreciatively. "Just you jiggers see you don't louse it up."

"If he's good enough for the Army to trust," Elveck reflected, "he ain't no jughead."

"Never said so, but he can't get anywhere without takin' a chance."

They ate, packed up the kitchen, then Hackett sent the pair on with the string. He led his own horse a little farther into the timber. He could see about half a mile of the trail from where he stopped, and he had a strong hunch that Dalton was not only dogging but was not far behind him. He waited patiently.

He was biting off a chew when his horse warned him by lifting its head. Hackett clamped its muzzle, lips peeled from his teeth while he watched the trail down-canyon. Then he frowned. Two riders had appeared, and in a moment he swore softly. They were Chinamen, riding flea-bitten mules. He cursed them silently while they passed and went on up the canyon, then he settled himself for another wait.

Nothing happened, although he remained there for two hours, growing cold from the inertia. He had lost some of his certainty that Nan would bait the trap. He cursed her, too, and promised himself retaliation if she had let him waste his time off here. He waited an hour longer, then mounted angrily and rode on after his packstring.

He didn't rush, and from time to time looked back, still nagged by the feeling that Dalton had to be following him. When he caught up with the string it had camped for the night, as ordered, in the mouth of Bumblebee Gulch, still several miles short of Steamboat.

"Nary a thing," he retorted grumpily to their looks of inquiry.

"Nan didn't do it," Elveck said with conviction.

"She had to," Hackett said doggedly. "She's as deep in the muck as we're in the mire, and she knows it. Moreover, I let her think it was Tremaine's wishes. She ain't got over him. She'd do what he wanted."

They cooked supper and night ran in. Hackett revised his estimate of the situation. Nan had baited him, but Dalton was too cagey to let himself be seen. Better man than Hackett had estimated. He accepted that and drew again on his own wily resources. He would have to carry his sham further than he had intended, to the point where Dalton would be compelled to take a long chance. By the time he rolled up in a saddleblanket and tarpaulin, Hackett had figured it out.

After the morning meal, he said, "Throw on the hulls, boys. We're goin' up to the old Bumblebee Mine." That was at the head of this canyon, a workings that had been abandoned a couple of years before.

They stared at him, but experience had taught them not to pry when he grew close-mouthed. Blankets and wooden saddles were cinched on the animals, then Hackett headed the string up the side canyon. Two miles farther they came to the old mines which had cost its operators a lot more than they got out of it. All that remained of the broken dream was a couple of tumbling shacks. The adit of the tunnel stared like a dead eye in the mountainside. Hackett swung down and went in.

He went no farther than daylight carried, then stopped, pulled out his plug and bit off a chew. He worked the wad leisurely, his jaded gaze on the rusting car tracks and other litter left because it was not worth moving out. Then he went outside.

"That'll do it," he said.

He led the string back down to the Applegate, then turned up its canyon toward Steamboat. But around the first bend, he pulled up and waved the men on. When they were out of sight, he dismounted and led his horse up the mountainside, then moved back along the slope above Bumblebee Canyon. When presently he sighted the old mine, he tied and left his horse. Five minutes later he was perched behind a rock above the mine shacks.

His stratagem bore fruit without the long wait of the day before that had produced nothing. When he saw the bay horse appear down the canyon, moving quietly and with its rider vigilant, Hackett chuckled and congratulated himself. Dalton had spied on his camp, last night. He had been puzzled by the movements this morning. Now he stopped a hundred yards below the first shack, ground-tied the horse and came on afoot. He had drawn a gun.

Hackett let him pass beneath him and come up to the adit. He let him go in and look around and enjoyed the bewilderment he had created. Then Dalton emerged and looked around, more puzzled than ever. He started toward one of the shacks to see if he could find anything more illuminating there.

Hackett's gun was firm in his grip when he shouted, "Turn around, army boy, with your hands empty and up!"

For a second he thought Dalton would make a fight of it, but he seemed to have good sense. He turned, letting the gun fall, lifting his hands. Hackett stumped down the slope to him, picked up the revolver and grinned.

"What's Uncle Sam gonna say about his bright boy now?" he taunted.

"Real smart," Dalton murmured.

"You're pretty foxy, yourself," Hackett conceded. "Wasn't sure till I seen you in the canyon that you'd took bait."

"Bait?"

Hackett laughed at him. "You think Nan was just makin' palaver?" He wanted Dalton to know just how he had been taken in.

Dalton said nothing, but his eyes were grim. Hackett told him to start walking and followed him down the slope. They picked up the bay, but he made Dalton keep walking until they had got his own horse from the sidehill. Then they mounted, with Hackett behind, his gun still fisted. He itched to use the weapon and be done with it, but Tremaine hoped to get something helpful out of the fellow.

Hackett rushed his prisoner, and they overtook the packstring before it had reached the scattered mining settlement of Steamboat. He savored the admiring glances of his men and turned them back down the Applegate.

"You boys go back to the J'Ville yard," he told them. "I've gotta hustle this fella to Gold Hill between now and daylight tomorrow."

"A reprieve?" Dalton said mockingly. "How come you're so merciful?"

"Boss wants to ask questions."

"Of me? What could I tell him he doesn't know already?"

"Don't try to throw sand, buck. You're the jigger the Army sent out from Missouri. Had us fooled a while, but after this —" He shrugged. "Get riding. We've got a far piece to go. And just you remember this. All I need to shoot you's a good excuse to give the boss. So don't give me one, if you want to live a while."

"Why the boss? I know you mean Tremaine."

"All right. Tremaine."

Had this been a man cut to his own principles, Hackett would have admired him. Dalton knew he was in the bind of his life, but it seemed to have done nothing but harden his face. His mistakes were excusable. He had had no reason to distrust Nan, whose only involvement with Tremaine as far as an outside could know, was of the heart. Nan had a way of winning people's liking. Her generosity and helpfulness had even, in many cases, won gratitude. Hackett was sure that this error of judgment bothered Dalton, more than did his walking into the trap at the Bumblebee.

Twice, riding down the river, they met oncomers, giving Hackett uneasy moments. But Dalton didn't gamble his life by trying to take advantage of it. Each time Hackett had to holster his gun, but he stood ready to use it before witnesses if pressed. Dalton would have made him face a firing squad, if he could have. He still would, if he got away and lived.

Night caught them on the rugged trail on Timber Mountain, for Hackett had decided to take the direct route to Gold Hill and bypass the other valley settlements. His worry increased as daylight faded. Finally he called a halt and lashed Dalton's hands behind his back and his feet under the belly of the horse. Thereafter he could lead the man's horse. Even so, he found himself looking back uneasily every few moments.

Chapter 12

He was at least seeing the one section of the Lady Luck, Tracy thought bleakly, that he had not already visited in secret. The gallery where the main tunnel and shaft joined was not large. In the smoky light of lanterns it seemed like a cave, although it was floored and fixed up for comfort far beyond that in a working mine. When he looked to the left, he could see into the outer length of the tunnel. At its end was a daub of the daylight Hackett, for all his hurrying, had beaten only by a few minutes.

Two men held Tracy, each with a solid grip on his arm, and others faced him in hostile amusement. Of these one was Hackett, whose triumphant arrival with his prisoner had caused a flurry of excitement and brought Tremaine hurrying into the mine.

"All right, Dalton," Tremaine said coolly now, "I'll ask you once more. Who have you taken into your confidence around here? Klippel? Old Abe? You might as well tell us first as last. We'll get it and a lot more out of you. One way or the other."

Hackett stirred, and Tracy sensed the eagerness in him to start the torture that so far had not been used. Tracy knew that his chances of leaving the mine, alive or dead, were less than slight. But he was resolved to leave them mystified, worried as to how close they were to disaster themselves.

Tauntingly, he said, "What you should worry about, Tremaine, is whether there's anyone who isn't on to you and waiting for you to convict yourself."

"Don't be clever," Tremaine snapped.

"Don't you be stupid. There are imponderables in everything, as you ought to know. You've come a long way from the pat security you had before the Piutes burned those wagons. You've got in deep. You're vulnerable in a lot of ways. You don't know who all knows as much about your rotten game as I do. You wouldn't have been sure of me, except for your ex-mistress. I'd suspect her of indiscretion. Not of treason. Or you'd still be in your fool's paradise."

"Leave her out of it."

"Oh, she's in, so deep she might destroy your marriage. I've a feeling you'd like to keep that. I would in your place."

"And leave my wife out of it."

Hackett said impatiently, "Want me to take the sass out of him?"

In an anger he had not betrayed until then, Tremaine said, "Go ahead."

Hackett grinned and came forward slowly. Tracy felt hands tighten on his arms, and the men holding them drew back, applying a pressure that hurt in itself. Yet he eyed the man before him with an indifference that wrenched Hackett's features out of their look of mockery. The beefy packet set to work with his big fists.

The first blow made a thunking impact under the breast bone. Tracy's mouth sagged open, while a searing pain exploded through his body. Hackett's iron-hard fists were slow, deliberate, and his shoulders swung and lifted each time he hammered that pain-swollen, excruciated spot. He struck half a dozen times before he finally stepped back.

Tracy sagged against the men who stepped in to hold him up. Distantly, he heard Tremaine saying, "Heroics will get you nothing, Dalton. There's nobody but us to see them."

"God — damn — you —"

"What names were on the list Fort Churchill gave you?"

"Nearly everyone in your — rotten organization."

"Don't give me that. Was mine? Hackett's? Groot's?"

"Everybody's — nobody's — you figure it out."

"He needs some more," Hackett said.

"Wait," Tremaine said.

Tracy could see a little better. Tremaine regarded him with bitter intensity, betraying a naked need to dominate him. Tracy held back the impulse to taunt him about the ammunition on the level below, almost under their feet. That would tip them off to the connecting drift, endanger Abe Jewett. He bit his lip.

"What's been done to offset us, Dalton?" Tremaine asked.

"Enough."

"Guess he don't like livin'," Hackett said. "He figures if he's gonna die, he might as well keep his mouth shut."

"I've got a choice?" Tracy asked.

"Between goin' easy and hard."

"Thought about — the consequences — if I disappear?"

"You ain't gonna disappear," Hackett retorted. "Somebody's gonna find your cayuse, back there on the Applegate. If they look hard, they'll find you. Scalped.

Mebbe you don't know there's still Injuns in the mountains around there. They'll lift hair, if they catch a white man alone."

Tremaine took it up, adding, "We aren't bluffing. There's no reason to. So make it easier on yourself."

"All right." Sickness was rising in Tracy's battered belly. "I'll talk. Some storm we had, wasn't it? Do you suppose it hurt the winter wheat?"

Hackett cursed and was on him, and Tremaine didn't stop him. That time the packer concentrated on Tracy's face, his head. The blows were staggering, blinding, for the man had given way to a completely unleashed fury. "Crisake, Hack!" somebody protested, as if at a great distance. The sledging kept on, and another voice said, "Hell, he's already out cold — !" and Tracy's legs were no longer holding him up.

"I'll kill him!" he heard Hackett fume. "What I should've done in the first place!"

"Stop it!" Tremaine said urgently. "And lay off. He'll talk. He's got to talk."

And that was the last Tracy knew . . .

The pain was the first to return, shooting like flame jets along his nerves. Enough awareness followed to tell Tracy he was stretched on the bare boards of the gallery floor. Nobody was talking, but he knew that if he moved they would jerk him upright and start in again. He no longer doubted their determination, the extent they would go to to learn what they wanted to know. Beating would be the mildest. There were things like hot wires under the nails, others even worse. If he could keep from moving his cramping, pain-wracked body, he might gain a little more time.

He managed it for a long moment in which there was no sound at all. His head cleared enough for him to wonder at the unnaturalness of that. His eyes felt too swollen to open, but he managed to pry the lids apart the merest slits. He was emboldened to turn his head. The lantern light showed him a space that was empty, except for himself. They had left the gallery, and he couldn't understand it. He turned his head and looked toward the adit. Daylight, out there, was now strong and full. He could make out two men, standing at the tunnel mouth.

When he began to understand, a ray of hope came alive. They had not found Abe's coyote hole in the old ore pocket. They thought the only way he could escape was through the adit, which they were guarding. They had all day to work on him, for they couldn't move his horse and body before nightfall. Some casual thing, like breakfast, had taken all but those two men away.

If he could still walk, Tracy knew his chances were good of slipping deeper into the tunnel and making his way to the ancient ore pocket. But the chances of their failing to find the coyote, after such an escape, were not good. That would bring Abe into it as a mortal danger to them, an open enemy, too. It would let them estimate more accurately how much was known about them and their preparations.

Tracy wanted to save his life, but it was not that which decided him. If these men carried out their plan to kill him, he would not be missed for some time. Klippel and Abe both knew he had gone to stalk Hackett up the Applegate. By the time they realized he had run into trouble, the mine could be cleared of its incriminating ammunition. He had to prevent that. Abe would want him to.

He managed to sit up, watching the lighted tunnel entrance until the pain had died down. Then he began to crawl backward, his eyes still on the distant guards. Neither so much as glanced back into the mine. He got over between the car rails and, inch by painful inch, craw-fished into the darkness, deeper in the tunnel. There he tried standing. A retching dizziness assailed him, but he braced himself against a timber, and it passed. He kept backing, thereafter, watching the entrance and feeling his way along the shoring. By the time he reached the drift that led to the pocket, he was in total darkness, reliant on his sense of touch alone.

He rested, then felt his way to the timber that concealed the connection with the Yellow Jacket. He was almost too weak to move the obstruction out of his way and, when he had crawled into the coyote, work them back in place. He finally managed it and rested again. Then he backed out of the coyote and a few minutes later stumbled into the lighted working face where Abe was busy with his crew.

They all turned toward him, and Abe gasped, "My God."

Tracy told him in gasping breaths what he had experienced. The prospect of drawing the wrath of the apparatus onto his own head did not trouble Abe one whit. He helped Tracy to the shack outside and there sponged his bruised and bleeding face and swollen belly with icy water. He worked silently, his shrewd eyes burning with anger.

By the time he was through, there was hot coffee on the stove, which he laced with whiskey and gave to Tracy. "We just could fool 'em," he commented. "Keep 'em wonderin' till the day they get shot how you got away."

Tracy gasped, "How?"

"By fillin' the back of that pocket with waste from my mine. Put in so much one man couldn't move it in a day's work. There's so many cave-ins in those old workings, they wouldn't know where to begin, even if they wondered if there was a inside connection. I'd say they'd figure you got out through the adit, in spite of their guards and what they claim. You okay for a while?"

"For a long while, thanks to that hole you dug me."

Abe nodded toward the rifle that stood by the door. "If you need that, she's loaded. But they won't look for you on the surface right off. Mebbe not inside, since they weren't in no rush to finish the job and might not miss you for a while. It won't take me and the boys long to fix that connection."

"Be careful, though."

Abe grinned. "Listen who's talkin'. Fix you some grub, if you feel like it. Help yourself to anything."

"Ugh," Tracy said.

But the fortified coffee had strengthened him, and Abe had enheartened him. His main hope was that Abe's role could be kept hidden from Tremaine and his hardbitten crew. He not only liked the old fellow. Abe and his men were assets that had helped and might prove useful again. Tracy refilled his cup, leaving out the whiskey, and sat drinking it while he pondered his next move. It had to be something to discourage Tremaine from removing the damaging ammunition, not only from the Lady but from his other mines.

Abe was back in less than two hours, looking satisfied. "We cut it," he reported. "Don't think they've found you missin', even. There's no big rumpus in the Lady, anyhow."

"They're giving me time to come to and sweat a while," Tracy reflected. "Abe, I'm going down to see Nan Bollinger."

"What for?"

"She got me into it, and she can help me get out. Besides, I wouldn't want Tremaine to find me with you before I've seen her."

"How're you gonna get down there in

broad day? Gotta go right past the Lady."

"Can't I slip down the other way, straight down to the river?"

"Could, but it's mighty rough."

"No rougher than the night I had."

Tracy got into his coat and stepped outside, making his way quickly around the shack and dropping into the slope timber beyond. He felt partially restored, although the painful, swollen contusions were a steady reminder that he had taken punishment. Some of the stiffness had worked from his body by the time he was down to the Rogue. Afterward, he followed a trail that led up to the old placers at Big Bar and came swiftly to Gold Hill from the river side.

No one was in the hotel lobby, luckily, for he did not want to be questioned about his beat-up face and bloody clothes. Nan could have been in the kitchen, but he took a chance on her being in her rooms, which she was. She answered his knock and gasped when she saw who it was.

"Oh, no!" she cried and lifted a hand to her mouth.

He shoved in and shut the door. Coldly, he said, "I thought better of you, Nan. I really did."

She turned and walked to the window.

When she swung around again, her face was as white as her shirtwaist. "There's no use denying anything," she said weakly. "But I didn't realize they'd hurt you. They wanted to see for sure if you're an army man. I guess I — wouldn't let myself think beyond that. I was afraid for myself."

"They meant to kill me. How deep are you in?"

Nan dropped slackly into a chair and covered her face with her hands. When she took the hands away, her eyes were stricken. "All the way now, I guess."

"You weren't before?"

"I suppose I was," she said miserably. "Far enough that I was frightened when Hackett said you were here to get us all shot. I didn't want to help him trap you, but I was scared enough to want to know if it was true. I didn't think beyond that. I should have. I wouldn't let myself, maybe."

"How much have they let you know?"

"Nothing, really, except what they want to do here."

"It would take more than that for you to be so frightened of your part in it."

"Well, I helped Alan meet the people he needed. I was well acquainted here, he wasn't. So — well, I helped him meet the ones I thought would listen to him."

"Want to give me their names?"

"Oh, Tracy," she said miserably. "Most of them have been good to me. I've been a traitor to my country. Don't ask me to betray my friends, now, just to save myself."

"All right. I know they have large stores of guns and ammunition, in addition to their local personnel. Do you know where the arms are hidden?"

Nan met his eyes. "I don't. Honest."

"Very well. I'm trying to believe you didn't want me killed or even beat up, but you'll have to help me believe it."

"Don't ask me to betray anybody else."

"Not even Tremaine?"

"You know about him and Hackett and those men at the mine."

"But I've got to know more," Tracy insisted. "Of utmost importance is where they've hidden the guns we know were smuggled into the country last summer and fall. Also when they intend to move. Get me something on that, and you've squared yourself, as far as I'm concerned."

She looked doubtful. "Alan doesn't come around, anymore, and I don't think the others have been told any more than I was. But I'll try. I promise you that."

Tracy left her room and went to his own, where he changed his clothes. When he glanced in the mirror, he didn't wonder that his appearance had given Nan such a shock. Maybe she hadn't realized what she was letting him in for, and maybe she would not try to help him. Yet it was not the hope of that which had led him to see her. He had wanted to impress her with the idea that he knew nothing of the exact location of the ammunition. Not only would that divert their attention from Abe Jewett. It might lull them into leaving the contraband where it was.

Chapter 13

Tremaine hesitated before he laid his hand on the knob of Nan's door. Then he opened the door and stepped boldly into a lamplit room, seeing Nan at the window, turning toward him, unsmiling.

He said awkwardly, "Hello, Nan. Your hostler was at the mine, today. He said you want to see me."

"I want very much to see you."

Tremaine had avoided her since he moved out of the room next to this one, the room with the connecting door. Yet, when there had been so much between them, it seemed absurd to meet now as strangers. But that was what she had become, he reflected while he studied her. She had drawn a cloak of reserve about herself that made her like someone he had never really known. He moved deeper into the room, and Nan's hand motioned toward a chair. He shook his head, not wanting to stay any longer than he needed. It was that completely over between them.

"So," Nan said, "you had your man involve me in what, without my knowing it, was to be a dirty murder."

"It was Hackett's idea," Tremaine said quickly. "I don't know why I listened to him." Resentment had replaced the panic which, earlier that day, had driven him in futile circles for several hours. He would not soon forget the feeling that assailed him when they discovered that Dalton had pulled a seemingly supernatural disappearing act. "Why? Did Dalton jump you about it?"

She smiled bitterly. "He had credited me, it seems, with more character than I have. He didn't explain how he got away from you and your cutthroat crew. What happened?"

"Sheer carelessness." Anger again stormed in Tremaine. "We left a couple of men to watch him. They thought he was unconscious and went out in the yard for air. He slipped out behind their backs." That was more conjecture than conviction with Tremaine, and, although the men responsible stoutly denied any lapse on their part, it was the only plausible explanation.

"What will you do now?"

"I don't know. Did he say what he's going to do?"

Nan shook her head. "No, but I know what I'm going to do if anything like that happened to him happens again."

Stunned, Tremaine said, "Like what?"

"Like telling your wife about you and me. And about your real business here, which I don't think she understands."

"Nan! You wouldn't!"

"Oh, wouldn't I?"

Tremaine felt sweat drip from his armpits. "But, Nan — he's not only a danger to the plan. He's a threat to us personally. Don't you understand that? To you, the same as the rest of us."

"Don't I know it? But he hasn't enough to move in yet. I knew that from his questions. He knows what you're up to, that you have the people and arms about ready. But he doesn't know who the people are beyond you and your so-called mine crews. He asked if I knew where you hid the guns and ammunition, which I don't."

Tremaine's face relaxed. "And?" he encouraged.

"That's all, except for when it's to be."

"Well," he reflected, "it isn't as bad as I thought. Is he going to do anything about getting — uh, abducted and so on?"

"He didn't say."

"It's probable he wouldn't," Tremaine

mused. "Sure he wasn't misleading you deliberately?"

With a dry smile, she said, "I don't always know when I'm being deceived, but Tracy Dalton didn't."

"Good. If he lets it slide, so'll we, and wait for the next move." Tremaine smiled at her, knowing he had to wheedle her out of her dangerous mood. "I've missed you, Nan. I hope you understand how it is."

"Except for one thing. How do you expect your wife to react when she finds out what you're up to?"

"I can make her understand." She wasn't mellowing, and on a burst of impulse, he said, "Once it's over, and the dust has settled, you and I can work something out, too."

Her mouth opened. She stared at him in bewilderment. "You mean to resume our — I suppose you'd call it an affair?"

"Why not?" he said and laughed.

It was a long moment before she spoke, then she murmured, "How rotten can you get, Alan? How rotten do you think I am?"

"Now, look —"

"Never mind. I've been your tool, although I didn't understand it that way when I was. I trusted you with everything, while you trusted me with nothing."

Uneasily, he said, "How do you mean?"

"Such as when this thing's to happen so I can quit worrying about my part in it."

"It won't be long."

"You said that months ago."

"It's closer now." Tremaine had begun to suspect that she had started fishing. She had been jilted, and she seemed to like Dalton, and maybe she wanted to redeem herself by helping him. "Well, I've got a lot to do. Good night."

She didn't bother to answer.

Tremaine rode back to the Lady Luck, pulled Hackett out of a bunkhouse card game and took him to the mine office. "Dalton doesn't know enough yet to worry us," he said and explained why he thought that. "But we're sure of him, now, and know that he and maybe others are watching us like hawks. We've got to change our plans."

"Which ones?"

"Concerning the guns. It's far too dangerous, knowing what we now know, to distribute them in advance. We'll wait till just before the jumpoff."

"Dunno," Hackett objected. "There's a lot of work in getting them things spread around to where they'll be needed. For so short a time, anyhow."

"We've got plenty of men, and you've got a lot of pack mules. And at that point secrecy won't be as important to us."

"Guess you're right," Hackett admitted. "How about Dalton's cayuse? It's still in the mine barn."

"Put it in Nan's stable during the night. I think he'll let that business drop, if we do, and it's the easiest way to get the horse off our hands."

"It's queer Dalton went to Nan with things we couldn't beat out of him."

Tremaine said easily, "He didn't tell her anything. He was hoping to bully information from her, since he had her dead to rights. What he was interested in tells us what he hasn't found out so far."

"Well," Hackett reflected, "if we don't do any more till the big day, and can keep him outta the mines, he can rack around as much as he likes. All it'll do is drive him loco."

On that basis, Tremaine tried to relax and while away the time that still must pass before he got the signal he so longed to receive.

Slowly the days passed, and they remained mild, as if the elements had exhausted themselves in one month of violence. Presently even the tatters of snow were gone from the flats and hills, and only the shiny peaks in the distance reminded of the storm. Finally, on his rides between Jacksonville and Gold Hill, Tremaine began to notice the tender green hint of buds on the abundant willows. He wasn't a nature lover, but this year he thrilled to the coming of spring.

Yet at times he worried without any apparent cause. Dalton was a dangerous, a very clever man. It was impossible to be sure of him. After his astonishing escape from the Lady, he had reappeared boldly and resumed his role as another mining man. In spite of that violent incident in the mine, the community remained unaware of impending danger. Its ignorance of what was going on reminded Tremaine that he could not be completely sure, himself.

And Nan had left a thought in his mind that kept bothering him. He had to prepare Lorna for coming events. But could he actually win her to his way of thinking? It would be best to lead up to it gradually, yet he never found an inviting place to start.

Then one evening she said, "I wonder why we haven't seen anything of Tracy Dalton."

"Busy, I suppose," Tremaine offered.

"Why don't you ask him to dinner with

us? I should think you two could become great friends."

They were by the fireplace, and he had been reading the week's issue of the *Sentinel.* He lowered the newspaper to his lap and regarded her.

"How come you like him so well?"

Lorna looked up quickly from her sewing. "He's nice. And he's very interesting. Besides that, you know, he stood me in a good stead once."

Tartly, Tremaine said, "Where I failed you."

"I never thought that," she said, surprised. "At least, not after you explained it. But it was disconcerting to cross a thousand miles of desert and not be met. He was understanding, and —" She broke off for a moment. "You don't approve?"

In a curt voice, Tremaine said, "He doesn't impress me the way he did you. I'd rather not cultivate him."

She looked at him, astonished, perhaps thinking he was jealous. Then she shrugged and let the matter drop.

Yet it was an opening from which he could proceed to explain why he and Dalton could never meet again except as mortal enemies. He tried framing some remark by which he could get started. But would she understand his change of heart and sides in the war? Would she look the same way he did on his glowing prospects and enormous responsibilities? And how would he feel if he had to choose between them and Lorna?

Lorna had put down her sewing, and for moments she sat staring at the back of the newspaper Alan had again lifted between them. How naive she had been to suppose that joining him and forcing the issue would clear away the things that had mystified her since he left her in Cincinnati. In the weeks she had been in Jacksonville, trying to lose herself in the pleasure of at last running her own house, something had changed in either her mind or heart. For one thing, she admitted, she had grown thoroughly irritated by Alan's vagueness. She was no longer willing to have her natural curiosity put off or brushed aside. It annoyed her to hear him laugh and say that business was for men, frivolities for women.

Yet she hesitated to press him about his unexpected dislike for Tracy Dalton.

Her uneasiness was still with her the next morning, after Alan had left for Gold Hill to be gone perhaps several days. She tried to lose it in housework. He had wanted her to have a maid — which, out here, they called hired girls — but she had refused. Whatever their prospects, they weren't rich yet. Actually, Lorna didn't think she ever wanted to be very rich. She was too earthy, too plain and practical in her tastes, even if the accident of physical appearance made her seem more suited to expensive and elegant uselessness. She had met women in Jacksonville, no older than she, who already had several children. She envied them.

In midmorning she took her basket and walked the one block to California Street and the store where she did her marketing. The air smelled of spring, and the clerk who waited on her remarked on it, saying how pleasant the weather was for February. Then she stepped out to the street to come face to face with Tracy Dalton, who had been so much in her thoughts.

"Heavens," Lorna gasped. "We seem to have a way of bumping into each other in this doorway."

Yet that wasn't what had startled her so much as the appearance of his face. A yellow green under his eyes showed they had recently been blackened. There were scabs on his lips and both cheekbones, and she saw reddened areas where abrasions had healed.

"I ought to come by here more often," Tracy said. "How've you been?"

She thought he was genuinely happy to see her, and she wondered why it so pleased her to be talking with him. "Fine, thank you." He was brash, as he had shown with the thug who tried to rob him in Virginia City, and before her eyes was evidence of another such adventure or misadventure. In spite of herself, her mind linked this with what Alan had said about not caring to cultivate his acquaintance. It might be something scandalous, yet that did not fit her impression of Tracy. The impulse came to see how he, in turn, really felt about Alan. She added, "I should be provoked with you. We've expected you to call on us."

"We?" Tracy's gaze sharpened. "That includes your husband?"

There it was, her answer. The restraint of tactfulness was no longer strong enough to stop her question. Too much went on that was off-limits to her. She wouldn't put up with it any longer.

She said, "Have you had a fight?"

He shrugged. "Yes. Call it a brawl."

"Don't dodge me," she said severely.

"You were surprised that Alan would welcome you to our house. He's told me he doesn't care to cultivate you, if you want the truth. What happened? Did you have a fight with him?"

"Let's say he and I don't see alike, Lorna."

"What about?"

He held her gaze steadily. "You, for one thing, but we haven't quarreled over you. He doesn't know how I envy him his place in your life."

"Oh, Tracy," she said helplessly, her breath catching. She had liked his saying that, and she had less right to like it than he had to say it.

"I want you to know it. That there's nothing I care more about than your happiness."

"Tracy!" she gasped. "Is something going to happen?"

He only looked at her for a long moment, then touched his hat and went on along the sidewalk.

She went on to the butcher's, much more troubled now than before she had met him. She could remember nothing flirtatious in their casual but growing friendship, on her part or his. Naive as it now seemed, she had not stopped to think that it might affect him more deeply than it did her. She wondered if he considered her a flirt, when she was only impatient with many of the strictures laid on women who were supposed to be ladies. Alan understood that part of her, at least, or he would never have left her alone for so long, after only six months of marriage.

This was her first, feminine reaction to the incident, but by the time she got back to the house she could no longer put off examining her feeling that he had tried to prepare her for something. Something resulting from him, involving Alan, and her, as well. He had wanted her to see it in a light other than the one in which it would appear. He liked her a lot. Maybe he was in love with her. And yet he thought he would have to hurt her. Somehow he was pitted against Alan, in that maddening outer world she was permitted to learn nothing about. Yet it was preposterous that Alan could have inflicted physical punishment on Tracy without showing the effects himself. He wasn't big or tough enough for that.

It came to her with a shock that she was championing Tracy against her husband.

She did not pry at Alan during the next two weeks, in which he divided his time between home and Gold Hill. Then came the evening that only increased her bewilderment and mounting fears.

Alan left his horse at the livery, as was his habit on the nights when he was home. And according to her habit, she fled to meet him at the door at the sound of his steps on the porch. She saw he was in a high good humor, for some reason, since she was sensitive even to moods she did not understand.

But this one was to be explained, for he had barely kissed her when he said, "I take it you've been home all afternoon."

"Yes. Why?"

"There're some new bulletins at the *Sentinel* office." He walked with her to the parlor, his arm around her waist. Then, looking down into her eyes, he said, "Jefferson Davis has proclaimed Arizona to be Confederate territory. Confederate forces from Fort Bliss have occupied Tucson. A much larger force has struck north from the fort into New Mexico."

"Why, how ghastly! Alan, what does it mean?"

"How do I know?" he said and still watched her.

"You don't seem very alarmed about it. Good heavens, Alan. You haven't been out here long enough to lose your concern about the war."

Dryly, he said, "Hardly."

"You seem amused."

"Largely, I suppose, because it's got this town so frightened. They'll be forming home militia and drilling in the streets."

"You don't think there's any real danger?"

"I don't consider it a danger, darling."

"Well, I hope it isn't. Until General Grant took command on the Missouri, the people at home were afraid we'd lose the whole West. And I've heard talk about an attack coming from Texas, anyway. Alan, think what it would mean if we were overrun by Confederate troops. We'd be prisoners of war."

"Hardly," he said and laughed.

"Well, I'm glad you can treat it lightly, and I hope you're not trying to keep me from worrying about it."

Before supper was over, she knew this was not the case. Alan was still excited, and several times he seemed on the point of talking about it. Yet he did not.

And so it was for several days, in which his secret elation filled him, leaving her confused, unhappy, and sure that she did not know the man to whom she had tied her life. Sure that somehow, in coming here, she had forced her way into a situation she might better have stayed out of. Then, a week from the start of this strange development, the *Sentinel* appeared with banner headlines:

SIBLEY TAKES ALBUQUERQUE

The boy threw the paper on her porch in midafternoon, and Lorna hurried out to bring it in, dropping weak-kneed into a chair by the window. What she read was stark refutation of Alan's assurance that the Confederate general was no danger to them. The scattered Union forces in New Mexico, to this point, had hardly slowed the two thousand men marching up the Rio Grande valley. There had been a pitched battle at a place called Valverde, and now nothing stood between Sibley and Sante Fe, the territorial capital of New Mexico. The government was preparing to transfer itself to Las Vegas, farther out on the traders' trail Sibley must follow in his march on gold-rich California.

An editorial in the same issue tried, without conviction, to evaluate the situation and exercise a calmer influence on its readers. The Confederates' objective seemed clear: to occupy Colorado and enough of Wyoming to cut the central overland trail.

After that, a drive on the treasure regions of the Far West would be undertaken, in concert with one out of Tucson. But, said the writer, there were the militias of all the Western states and territories to stand against that assault. They were made up of valiant men, who while untrained in warfare would be fighting for their families, their homes. Californians occupied Fort Yuma and would challenge Hunter at Tucson. The Colorado militia was said to be concentrating at Fort Union, which Sibley would have to capture to carry out his ambitious plan.

Lorna dropped the paper to the floor, sick at heart. The forces involved seemed puny compared to the massive armies that threw themselves against each other south of the Potomac. That was highly illusory, for Sibley's theatre was a far-flung, thinly populated frontier, in relation to which his command was a horde. She did not understand the principles by which wars were fought, but even were she the feather-brained woman Alan liked to pretend, he would never convince her that the West was not in grave peril.

He came home early, carrying a copy of the same paper, which he had picked up on the way. The instant she saw his enlivened face, she knew they were going to have it out before they slept. She waited through supper, saying nothing about the news, giving him a chance to bring it up. He failed to mention it. She washed the dishes, tidied the kitchen, and when she went into the sitting room he was seated before the fire, a half-smoked cigar in his fingers. She took her usual chair across from him.

"I want to know what's reversed your emotions," she said. "Why the calamitous news of the past week has only made you happy. Really happy, I might add, for the first time since I came."

He puffed on the cigar, regarding her. Then he smiled. "It's past time," he said, his voice calmer than she had been able to keep her own. "Sibley's proved they can't stand against him. And when he's taken Fort Laramie, my dear, I move to take the coast."

It was a while before her throat muscles relaxed enough for her to gasp, "You? Alan, are you mad?"

He told her, then, how in his river years, when he had been much in New Orleans, he had made close friends with men who now were important in the new nation fighting for its right to exist. How gradually his sentiments had changed until he began to see the injustice of a federal government that blindly and arrogantly overrode the rights of the states that gave it being. How, when he was asked to serve in the new cause, he had agreed, with the great need for secrecy preventing his explaining himself to her until now.

"It's treason — treason —" she gasped.

"Nonsense. It's military strategy. It's humane, because it will save hundreds of thousands of lives."

"How?" she said scornfully.

He tossed the cigar into the fire and leaned forward, his eyes burning with a zeal she had never seen in them before. "The war's been on a year, and the Union forces haven't been able to get off dead center. George McClellan talks big plans, but his performance is no better than his predecessors'. Why? There's no real will to fight us in the North. And the loss of the West will destroy what little there is. Our side will be much the larger, with the West won for it. We'll have the mineral wealth they now have and will miss sorely. They'll be happy then, my dear, to leave us alone and look to their own survival."

"You're a traitor to the people here who've trusted you."

Alan laughed easily. "This will surprise you, since your interests haven't ranged far outside your home. If the federal authorities dared to hold a plebiscite, and let the West choose the government it wants over it, they might lose it to us that way. Nobody knows, of course, but I assure you, there'll be about as many who will regard me as a great leader as those who will consider me a traitor."

"I guess," she said dully, "this accounts for the feeling between you and Tracy Dalton."

"He's an undercover man from the Army. We suspected it from the start. Recently we proved it."

"You're responsible for his being beaten up."

His eyes narrowed. "How did you know about that?"

"I saw him. However, he didn't tell me what happened."

"It had to be done. We had to learn how much is known of our plans and preparations."

"Did he tell you?" she asked coldly.

He shook his head.

"You'll have to shoot your way into power, of course," she said. "How many lives do you expect it to cost here, while you're saving them elsewhere?"

His glance sharpened. "No more than necessary. But this is war, Lorna. You've got to understand that. You're shocked now, which is understandable. I'm sure your attitude will change, when you've had time to think."

"You're making me a traitor perforce. Why did you give me no choice, Alan?"

For the first time he was angry. He got to his feet. "Use that word, if you must. But, my dear, be sure you use it only with me. You understand why, don't you?"

Wornly, she said, "They shoot traitors."

"Exactly, and from the Northern viewpoint I'm treasonable. It will be so, and don't you forget it, till the government out here changes and I become a patriot, which I am."

She rose, too, and faced him with level eyes. "You're making me choose between my conscience and my love for you. Maybe there's a way out of that."

Frowning, he said, "How?"

"Suppose I make you choose between me and your ugly ambition?"

What remained of her heart came apart while he stood silent and suddenly remote.

Chapter 14

The punch of a rifle shook the timber, and the bay horse reared straight up, pawing air. Nearly unseated, Tracy flung a glance at the sidehill above just as a second shot aroused the echoes. The sound of this bullet snapped in his ears, proving the deadliness with which, somewhere in the canyon, somebody was aiming. He whipped the bay behind a boulder and swung it to a stop, his revolver fisted.

There were no more shots from above him. Tracy leaned forward to pat the neck of the horse, which still snorted and strained to get moving. He saw blood. The first shot had clipped hair and skin from the animal's neck, close to the head. Whoever it was had tried for his horse, more than him, hoping to put him afoot, perhaps to capture him.

He had scared up something, at last, although he still didn't understand it.

He had been coming up a creek fringed by leafless willows, poking into a digitate valley at the upper end of Bear Creek. He had learned of Hackett's ranch, up here, sometime before, yet it had been a while before he tumbled to its possible significance. He was on a back part of the ranch, as yet, which he had approached in a roundabout manner. So they had been keeping tabs on him since his escape from Tremaine's mine. This was the first time they had betrayed the fact, and he hoped the shots meant he was getting closer to something than they liked.

He swung down and tied the horse in the creek brush, knowing he could not ride out of there unseen. Thereafter he ran in a crouch along the creek for nearly a hundred yards, moving upstream. Then he was able to swing left through natural cover and across the narrow valley and get into the slope timber. Afterward he started back to where he guessed his attacker would be. He walked slowly, quietly, the rankness of the spring warmed earth rising about him. The only other movement was once when a bird slashed across the daylight above him.

His brush with death in the Lady Luck had relieved him of the need to keep up a pretense with his enemies. That had let him move more freely, which had helped, although they had countered his slipping from their hands by themselves suspending action. Even Hackett was loafing, killing time on his ranch, giving Tracy no chance to catch somebody at something that might help him solve the puzzle.

So Tracy had been forced to guide his search by certain logical assumptions. The illegal firearms would have to be stored where there was a minimum risk of discovery. They had to be sheltered against the elements, since rust would damage if not ruin them. That suggested a mine, a natural cave or a building. The first and last would have to belong to somebody connected with the seditious apparatus. Klippel had told him that there were some large caves on the head of Sucker Creek, over in the Illinois basin. But, being celebrated curiosities, they were often visited and would be a dangerous place to hide contraband.

So by slow elimination, Tracy's suspicions had finally settled on the ranch where Hackett took care of his pack animals. It lay in the valley of one of the many streams entering Bear Creek and was handy to the emigrant road. Hackett's pack outfits were in and out continually, with some of his crew on hand at all times. He had buildings on the place, and there could even be some old prospect hole on the property.

It would be as difficult to search Hackett's buildings as it had been to enter the Lady Luck in stealth. While still dangerous, it would not be impossible to explore the canyons in the packer's neighborhood and determine or eliminate the existence of a tunnel or shaft where some miner had tried his luck. Now here he was so promptly discovered Tracy knew he had been watched and perhaps trailed. He had turned the tables in Virginia City, walked into a sucker trap on the Applegate, and in a moment he would know which he was going to do again.

A little while later he stopped dead still. Down from him a man was crouched behind a rotting log while he scanned the area below. He held a rifle, and on beyond in the trees was a saddle horse with dropped reins. The horse wore Hackett's burned H on its shoulder. The man was watching the area where the bay horse had cut from sight. Tracy did not recall having seen him before.

He moved quietly toward him, expecting the Hackett horse to betray him at any moment. He was within fifty feet, however, when he let his voice break the silence.

"Drop the rifle, and get your hands up fast!"

Reflex jerked the man erect, and he seemed on the point of whipping the rifle around. Tracy's gun jarred against his hand, the bullet spanged on metal, and the fellow dropped the rifle, shaking his stung fingers and cursing bitterly.

"If I'd been you a while ago," Tracy said, "I wouldn't have missed a thing as big as a horse's head." He moved down, bent and picked up the rifle. Still holding the revolver on his captive, he stepped back. "Now, my friend, you and I are going to Jacksonville to see the sheriff."

"What — what for?" the man sputtered.

"Attempted murder."

"Look, mister. I got orders. There's scum travels the California road. We lose stock to 'em all along. Horses, mules. That's what I reckoned you were up to. Only tried to scare you off."

"You know who I am, and what I'm doing here. What's your name?"

The man hesitated, swallowed, then said, "Tanner. Pete Tanner."

"What do you do for Hackett?"

"Wrangle. Work around the ranch. Things like that."

"You followed me from Jacksonville this morning."

Tanner dropped his gaze. "All right. But it won't do you no good to take me to the sheriff. There ain't nothin' I'm gonna tell him, because I don't know nothin'. I just do what they tell me."

"Your latest orders being to kill or capture me. Right?"

"If you've got the answers, why bother with the questions?"

Tanner was a hard case and it would not be easy to break his nerve and make him talk. Tracy regarded him in cold distaste, discarding the idea of taking him in for a sweating.

"How far are we from ranch headquarters?" he asked.

Tanner nodded down the canyon. "Couple of miles, mebbe."

"Take off the boots."

"Hey —"

"Get 'em off," Tracy snapped.

Tanner's lips muttered profanely while he obeyed. Tracy picked up the boots and, still carrying the rifle, backed up the hill toward Tanner's horse. When he reached the animal, he threw the reins over its neck, the stirrups across the saddle, then gave it a whack.

"Throw dirt!" he shouted.

The startled animal bolted down the slope, crashed into the brush, and a moment later appeared on the canyon floor at a full gallop. Ignoring Tanner's yells, Tracy followed down. When he reached the creek, he tossed the rifle and boots into the water. In a couple of minutes he was mounted on his own horse and following Tanner's down the canyon.

It would take the tender-footed hard case an hour to reach headquarters and raise an alarm. Before that happened, Tracy wanted to finish his search of the area. He soon came into the main valley of the creek on which Hackett had established his ranch. He turned up this valley and twice within the next hour inspected a draw without finding anything of interest. He crossed at the head of the valley and began to work his way down toward headquarters, the time in which he could do so in reasonable safety about run out.

He still had found nothing when he came to a viewpoint that let him see the ranch buildings, hardly a quarter of a mile away. At this distance he could see no activity there, the view being somewhat broken by trees. Nor could he see anything of Tanner, picking his slow way barefoot.

Tracy sat his saddle in deep thought, denying himself the cigar he craved. Word of Sibley's almost unimpeded march on Colorado had nearly shocked him into ordering the immediate seizure of the known plotters and ammunition caches. The factor that had stopped him previously inhibited him again. He could not gamble; he had to make sure he had broken the back of the proposed uprising. That would be all the more important, if Sibley succeeded in cutting off the Far West.

He thought he had achieved something now, in spite of Tanner's interference. Hackett's own position made him susceptible to panic. The fact that suspicion had centered on his ranch might jar him out of his inactivity, if the guns really were hidden somewhere on it. Tracy swung his horse back onto the ridge, descended on the far side, and came out into Bear Creek's valley. A little later he was following the stage road toward Jacksonville, to which he had moved. The valley metropolis was more central to the area he now suspected of concealing the rest of the contraband.

He left the horse at the livery barn. Going on toward his hotel, he found depressing news on the *Sentinel* bulletin board which, after stage time each day, now drew a bigger crowd than any other attraction in town. The rebel force out of Fort Bliss had occupied Santa Fe, with the territorial government of New Mexico having fled to Las Vegas. There was worry in the faces of the men standing about, the irrepressible gleam of an inner eagerness that identified the Southern sympathizers.

For a week thereafter, Tracy spent long and wearing days keeping a close watch on Hackett's ranch headquarters. To his increasing puzzlement, there was no attempt to interfere with him, and no sign that his prowling had thrown Hackett off stride or frightened him in the least. During the entire period, no packstring came or left the ranch. Several times he saw the packer himself at a distance, proving he was still there. That forced Tracy to conclude he had either failed to stir the packer sufficiently to worry him or had followed a false lead. Tracy began to see the discouraging prospect of starting all over again.

On a Saturday night, when Jacksonville was its most crowded with miners and country bloods in for a good time, Tracy sat in his hotel room, again tempted but still reluctant to move in on Tremaine. Then he lifted his head, listening to a rap so light it seemed to be down the hallway from his door. It came again, the merest touch on the panel. He climbed to his feet and went over. When he opened the door, Nan Bollinger stood there, looking extremely nervous.

She stepped in hurriedly, and he closed the door, waiting until he had done so to say, "Hello, Nan. Is something wrong?"

"Oh, no." Then she smiled wearily. "That is, nothing is worse than it was the last time I saw you."

"Sit down."

"I'll only stay a moment." She looked keenly at his face, which no longer carried the evidence of her betrayal of him, a fact that seemed to ease her. She said quietly, "You asked me to find out things for you. I haven't been able to. But I remembered something I owe it to you to tell you."

"Maybe," he said gently, "you only owe it to your conscience."

"I guess that's it," Nan admitted. "It might not help you. But I don't think what you want's in the valley. Last fall Alan was on the desert quite a while and —"

There was no warning sound in the hallway, nothing at all until the door exploded inward and Hackett stood there. His eyes held a glitter as he strode through, swinging the door closed again with a jar that flickered the lamp flame. His high, wide frame was springy tense. The way he regarded Nan disclosed that she, at least, had shaken him out of his complacency.

Bitterly, he said, “You bitch.”

Tracy’s voice slapped him. “Cut it out, Hackett, and get out of my room.”

“You bitch,” Hackett said again in his dull, deadly voice. “Thought when I seen you come into this hotel it’d be smart to check up.”

Apparently he had been in town seeking pleasure, like most of the other visitors, but now a killing rage controlled him. Tracy’s fear was for Nan, not what the man could do to her here, but afterward. Hackett had listened at the door. He knew she had been about to reveal something, and there was no sense in trying to deny that she had.

Tracy said again, “Get out of my room, Hackett.”

The man swung on him, his eyes raking and contemptuous. “Uncle Sam’s gumshoe,” he intoned. “Heard you were out to the ranch a while back. How come we ain’t seen you since?”

“You haven’t looked for me.”

Hackett laughed. “We haven’t, because you can go over that ranch with a comb and not find a thing. You ain’t gonna get anything out of this loudmouth, either. Not that she didn't want to spill her guts. Till now, anyhow. Now you ain't going to, are you, Nan? Ever?"

She watched him steadily but did not reply.

Hackett's bullying eyes ran over her again, indecent in their lingering. "Cat got your tongue, bitch?" he said finally. "I asked a question."

It was the third time he had used that word on Nan, one more than Tracy could stand. Before he knew it, he struck, his fist driving wind out of Hackett's belly. Nan moaned a protest that Tracy ignored. Gagging, Hackett staggered backward, shoving out with both hands, trying to gather his wits, to get his breath and balance.

"Nobody holding you," Tracy murmured. "You've got a better deal than you gave me in the mine."

He crashed through the man's dazed defense and hit him again, his fists alternating in thudding impacts against the man's breast bone and under it, the place where Hackett had hammered him into sick unconsciousness. Hackett crashed into the wall, then his knee drove upward into Tracy's crotch.

It was vicious, merciless, and drove Tracy back. But Hackett was helpless, himself, gaping, his glazed eyes blindly searching. Tracy fought back the pain and drove forward again, but now Hackett was better prepared. A hickory-hard fist propelled Tracy back against the window noisily shattering the glass. Tracy fought for balance, on the point of going out, hearing Nan's scream. Echoing shouts came from below stairs. He caught his balance in time to duck aside, clear of the packer's charge. Hackett barely saved himself from a headlong dive through the window. Before he could haul around, Tracy was back on him.

Hackett bent over, trying to cover his face. A chair went over while he backed away. Tracy caught him on the nose with a looping fist. Blood spurted, the packer groaned. Afterward, Hackett could not escape the fists that completed the ruin of his face. He broke and drove blindly for the doorway. Men had gathered in the hall but had been afraid to interfere. Hackett headed for them, snorting blood, shaking his head. Tracy caught him short of the exit and swung him around. The blow that dropped him was like the whack of a club on meat. Hackett did not stir.

His breathing noisy in his throat and lungs, Tracy looked at the bystanders. One was the hotel clerk. "Find his friends," Tracy panted. "Get him out of here."

"What the hell happened?" one of them asked.

"A private matter. Come on, Nan."

She looked at him bleakly, then followed him past the gallery, to the stairs and down. Tracy was groggy, still half sick from the kick in the groin, but one thing was clear to him. Nan's life was not worth a wooden nickel now, whether or not she finished what she had started to tell him. She was his first concern.

The lobby had been emptied by the racket upstairs. Tracy stopped there, asking "How did you get here from Gold Hill?"

"The afternoon stage," Nan said. "I'm staying overnight."

"You were," he corrected. "And you can't go home, Nan. Not while that bunch is running loose."

"I've no place else."

"But you have. Till the dust's settled, you're going to be at Camp Baker. I'm taking you there right now. Eighty militiamen around you are none too many to suit me."

She knew her effort to redeem herself could have cost her life. She nodded. "And I hadn't much to tell you," she said dismally. "Little beyond what I did. That Alan was on the desert for a week or so, last summer. He mentioned it because he got a dreadful sunburn. He implied he was prospecting. I thought of that yesterday and wondered if the firearms you're hunting are out there, somewhere."

"I've wondered myself," Tracy said. "But it's a huge area. Did he give you any idea of where on the desert he was?"

"I'm sorry." Nan shook her head.

Tracy hurried her to the livery stable to hire a horse and buggy. He had to get her away, lost in the country and the night, before Hackett's crew learned what had happened.

Chapter 15

Tremaine had ridden out the double doors of the livery barn when Hackett's man hailed him. Turning in the saddle, he saw Satch Harmon, who did the blacksmith work on the ranch, riding toward him. Disliking open contact with that hardbitten bunch, Tremaine frowned. But the urgency in Harmon's manner caused him to rein around and wait for him to ride up.

Harmon said quietly, "Hackett wants you at the ranch."

"Why?"

"Well," Harmon said, with a hint of relish, "for once he bit off more than he could chew." He glanced along the quiet, morning street and dropped his voice still further. "It's the Bollinger woman. Hack caught her with Dalton at the Robinson house, last night. She was spillin' things to him."

"What?" Tremaine said, on a tight breath.

"That's what Hack wants to talk to you about. He'd of come to see you, but he's got a busted nose and mebbe some cracked ribs. He's roarin' like a bear with piles, this morning."

"Get to the point, damn it. What happened?"

"Virg Gotch was watchin' the hotel, keeping tabs on Dalton the way Hack ordered. Virg seen Nan go in and rushed off to find and fetch Hack. Nan was in Dalton's room. Hack listened a minute and heard her sayin' somethin' about the desert. He busted in and stopped it."

"How'd he get hurt?"

"There was a ruckus. And them that seen the finish say Dalton was hardly marked. But him and Nan disappeared, so she's still talkin', and God knows who to by now."

"Let's go," Tremaine said furiously.

They rode quietly out of town so as not to arouse curiosity, but once beyond the outskirts they lifted their horses to top speed. As fastidious as he was proud, Tremaine did not care for the company of his smelly, tobacco-spitting companion, nor for Hackett's, but this was something he had to investigate. He had tried not to worry about Nan, with whom he had abandoned wisdom for the sake of passing pleasure. He had discounted the damage she could do, although he had left her disgruntled and unhappy. But what had she told Dalton about the desert? She knew nothing about that, at least nothing that she had learned from him, and that was a very sensitive area.

Even with fast riding, it took nearly two hours to reach the clutter of shacky buildings and pole corrals that made up the headquarters of Hackett's ranch. Hackett was in the unpainted, barracks-like structure that served as a house. He only stared at Tremaine out of swollen eyes, not rising from the sagging leather couch on which he had propped himself with dirty pillows. He was holding a wet cloth to his nose and mouth, and Tremaine gasped when Hackett took the hand away.

Yet, after over-exposure to Hackett's insolence, his humiliation was as gratifying to Tremaine as it seemed to have been to Harmon. Tremaine said, "So you don't do so well without your boys to hold him."

In their pits of charcoal, Hackett's eyes were red as live coals. He cursed Tremaine, then put the soggy cold rag back to his nose, shaking his head. He said, "The son of a bitch had a length of pipe stashed in his room. How was I to know that?"

"How long had Nan been there before you arrived?"

"What does that matter? They've run together ever since. The boys spent the night tryin' to run 'em down. They're not in J'Ville, not in Gold Hill, and do you know what I think? Dalton's takin' Nan down to the army headquarters right now."

"She couldn't tell them much."

"Then where'd she get this desert business?" Hackett hooted. "I think when you were playin' cozy with her, you run off at the mouth."

"I told her nothing about the desert."

"She's just guessin'?" Hackett shut his fiery eyes and groaned. "This goddam nose is killin' me."

"I don't know where she got that," Tremaine insisted.

"If she gets the Army scourin' the desert with enough men, you'll wind up in a coffin instead of the governor's chair. And you'll take me with you."

"They haven't anything but suspicions, damn it," Tremaine retorted, aware that Hackett, if not handled skillfully, could give him a bad time, himself. "They know they can't make arrests without evidence. And they can't get enough evidence in the short time left."

"You don't know how much they have, and you've got to see they don't get more."

"How?"

"By jumping off. Right now."

Tremaine stared. "That's completely out of the question. Smarter men than you worked out the time table. If we don't do our part when and how we're supposed to, we could foul up the whole operation."

"You give Dalton time, and we're the ones fouled up. He was pokin' around my ranch all week. I let him do it to waste his time. Now he knows it was a waste, and he's got Nan to tell him God knows what that you let slip. Women are smart about addin' things up."

The packer's stewing fears were taking hold in Tremaine, draining off some of his confidence. But the way to meet the emergency was not to move hastily and unwisely, as Hackett suggested.

"Get hold of yourself, Hack," he said sternly. "I've no idea what Nan's up to, but she can't tell enough to stop us. However, you'd better send out a man to warn the boys on the desert. There's enough of them, out there, to stop Dalton and half a hundred others."

"When're we gonna get the word to light the fuse?" Hackett complained.

"When Sibley's ready to give it. Things will move so fast, after that, that they can't keep up with us, let alone catch up."

Tremaine walked out to his horse with more hope than assurance that he had calmed the unpredictable and often wholly reckless packer. Riding back toward Jacksonville, he reminded himself that he had to expect the unforeseen, like the wagons burned by the Indians and the accidental death of Joe Sanders in Virginia City. Nan's defection was of a kind like that, and there might be more of the same before this was over.

The following week did nothing to allay the uneasiness that remained in Tremaine. Nan did not reappear in Gold Hill, and the hotel help was as mystified as he as to what had become of her. Dalton had not given up his room at the Robinson House, yet nobody had seen him around Jacksonville since the night the pair vanished. But Tremaine did learn that Dalton had rented a buggy that night, and had driven east with Nan. That indicated that Hackett could be right about Dalton's taking her to the Army's Pacific headquarters, in California. If so, the military had not been sufficiently impressed to do anything. Nothing happened locally, and no word came of suspicious activities on the desert.

Meanwhile Tremaine grew increasingly pessimistic about winning Lorna to his support. After the night in which he disclosed his true purpose in the West, she had only withdrawn from him, refusing to let him argue, wheedle, or let him try to win her around through his affection. She kept a neat but perfunctory house, cooked adequate but uninspired meals, talked casually about his day and hers and the weather. She never went further than that, nor would she permit him.

It began to anger him finally, and one night he said insistently, "Can political convictions mean so much to you that you'd let them come between you and your husband?"

"I have no political convictions," she said quietly. "Only moral ones."

"What's that supposed to mean?"

"You don't know the distinction?"

"Not the ones you seem to be making."

"Then it wouldn't help to explain."

He had the disturbing experience of seeing her for an instant with Nan's face superimposed. He had always thought highly of his knowledge of women, of his ability to handle them, yet there had been a point beyond which he had known neither Nan nor Lorna in the least. Nan had gone over to the other side, but it had seemed incredible that Lorna could do the same. She was his wife, she loved him, which she had proved by coming so far to be with him against every discouragement. She couldn't want a part in causing his death, even if Nan had reached a point where she did. He could be sure of that much. In time, when he was a great man, Lorna would see how right he had been in this.

And then came the day when he reached home to find her strangely elated, although no different toward him than she had been of late. The hope rose in him that she had at last accepted things. It kindled an unexpected gaiety in himself.

"It's been a beautiful day," he said. "Been out in it?"

Lorna shook her head.

"Well, spring will bloom fast, now that March is gone," Tremaine offered. "Why don't you ride out to the mine with me, tomorrow? The countryside's beautiful now."

She looked at him strangely. "You didn't hear the news downtown?" She smiled. "I'm surprised. They even got out an extra."

"I wasn't downtown." He had left his

horse at the blacksmith shop on the edge of Jacksonville to have a shoe tightened. He had walked directly home from there. Something in her expression made him add sharply, "What's the news?"

"Your friend Sibley has been beaten badly and turned back. He's even lost his supply trains. He'll be lucky if he can get back to Texas."

"What?"

"The paper's over there," she said. "Read it for yourself."

The special edition of the paper lay on the center table, a small handbill scarcely more elaborate than the bulletins regularly posted on the board. He seized and began to read it, hearing the thunder of blood in his head. Lorna had not exaggerated. He uttered a shattered, "No!" as the black lines drew his eyes.

The Union forces falling back from Sibley's advance up the Rio Grande had, it was now revealed, concentrated at Fort Union in what must have been a calculated withdrawal. There they had been joined by Colorado militia until they formed a force half again the size of Sibley's. These, under Canby, had been lying in wait when the Confederate general, putting Sante Fe behind, started to cross the mountains and enter eastern New Mexico.

Two battles had been fought at Apache Canyon, short of the pass, with the Union losses light and the Confederates suffering heavy casualties. But the back-breaking blow had come when, while holding Sibley in the canyon, a Union detachment succeeded in finding and destroying his supply trains. Afterward, the reeling Sibley had fallen back to Sante Fe, so badly mauled he had no choice but to withdraw from the invaded territory, if that was possible.

And that was not all, Tremaine read to his horror. California militia, out of Fort Yuma, had swung from a defensive to an offensive posture and struck east across the desert toward Tucson. Already they stood in strength where Hunter could not hope to get around them and drive into Nevada. Hunter's force had been discovered to be small, no more than a company. The prediction was that he, too, would be driven back to Texas on the double.

Tremaine dropped weakly into a chair, crushed the paper and threw it into the fire. It was incredible that so strong a barrier could be raised from the confusion, complacency and lack of fighting spirit counted on to deliver the West to the

South. Men like Dalton were responsible, he thought angrily, men who had known more than they revealed, who had done more than they let out, who had planned more than seemed possible.

He grew aware that Lorna had left the room and realized he had not seen her leave. His anger lashed out at her, now, at the smile she had worn while she waited for him to see his world come down in ruins. Who was she to talk of loyalty? She had not only refused to accept her husband's views as reasoned and necessary to him, she had labeled them false and shown her scorn and, now, her mockery of them.

He had no idea how much time had passed when her voice said with a kindness that surprised him, "Supper's ready, Alan."

Tremaine glanced up and saw her in the archway. There was a faint concern, rather than triumph, in her face. She had grown sorry for him, not that it had happened but because he had suffered a deep disappointment.

He rose, followed her in and seated her, then walked around the table and sat down at his own place. They unfolded their napkins without speaking; he carved the roast and served. Her cheeks had colored. He had not the least appetite, but pride kept him from letting her see it. He made himself eat, then she picked up a fork and began to eat, too. Suddenly she laid the fork on the edge of her plate.

"Alan?"

"Yes, my dear?"

"It's a blessing in disguise."

"I quite agree, Lorna."

"You — agree?"

"Quite."

"Oh, thank God." She looked at him with brimming eyes. She began to smile.

"It's all the more important, now," Tremaine said harshly, "that I do my work with what I hope surpasses Sibley's competence." Her face sagged. She said nothing. "And, from a personal point of view, it's to my advantage that he failed so miserably. My achievement will have all the more lustre."

"You — you're going ahead?" she said weakly.

"Of course. I never thought otherwise."

"To succeed where Sibley failed." Lorna nodded. "To deliver the West, when all seemed lost. Yes, it will make you an even greater hero, Alan."

Mildly, he said, "There's nothing wrong in wanting stature."

"And power."

"They go together."

"You can't do it. Any more than Sibley could. People don't lie down to be walked over, even by conquering heroes. You'll only waste a terrible lot of lives."

Tremaine laughed. "We're not an army that's still hundreds of miles from its objective. We're on the spot. We're armed. We're prepared at a moment's notice to seize power. We're strong enough to put down local resistance. We have only a few mountain passes to defend to seal ourselves off until reinforcements can arrive. If not by land, then by sea. Sibley's defeat has freed my hand. I can act on my own, when I like. I can't fail, my dear, even if it distresses you to hear me say it."

"Loyal men are working against you here, the same as they did against Sibley. Tracy Dalton — you said, yourself —"

"We'll move," Tremaine said contemptuously, "before he can do a thing more than he's already accomplished. Which, I feel confident, is very little."

Wanly, she said, "And what will you be afterward?"

"If I retrieve Sibley's failure, I can have whatever I ask." He smiled at her. "With you my lady. My very great lady. You think that doesn't mean anything to you now.

But it will. You'll be surprised at how quickly you'll develop a taste for place and power and wealth."

"You seem very sure of me, Alan."

"I've seen others make your struggle. It's a natural one. You were raised on chauvinistic nonsense, the same as I was. You haven't learned how much injustice, corruption and self-interest it's designed to cover up."

"There's a great deal I've failed to understand," she agreed.

"You're mocking me."

"No. I'm just realizing that you're quite sincere in your feelings."

"Because I refuse to accept defeat?"

"It shows how strong they are. The naked, ruthless vanity, the ambition that hasn't a shred of high principle in it. I wonder if I had company in my blindness. The people who sent you here. The ones already here who are willing to give their lives because of genuine ties with the South. I wonder if they understand that you are working strictly for the aggrandizement of Alan Tremaine."

He crumpled his napkin, tossed it on the table, and shoved back his chair. She sat watching with an almost hypnotized attention, her lips parted while she weighed and considered him. He walked to the hall and took down his sheepskin and hat. He went back to the dining room door and saw her still sitting there, looking straight ahead.

"I might not be back for a while," he said.

"Not to sound the bugles?" she asked.

Furiously, he said, "Look, Lorna. You can't prevent this. I'd much rather have you with me. But even with you against me, I'm going ahead."

He went out into the night.

Two hours later he was closeted with the men in the mine bunkhouse at Gold Hill, their hard, bold faces reassuring him. The news he had himself learned only that evening had not reached them until he divulged it. Thus their dismay at Sibley's surprising defeat was quickly cancelled by his announcement. Their plans would go forward with increased vigor, he told them, now that it all depended on them.

Bide Tugwell raised the only question. "How about the outsiders who've said they'll come in with us? This gonna make 'em lose heart?"

"Some of them," Tremaine admitted. "Until we've proved we can put it over on our own. You see Hackett, Bide. Tell him to ram through the guns, whatever the risk.

George, you tell the boys on the desert. I want you to go to the Comstock, Frank, and post Groot. Come back by the Yuba and set it up there. Larry can see Jimson at Waldo. They all have detailed plans and only need the date."

Tugwell grinned. "So what's the date?"

"A week from today."

"Where'll you be?"

"Here or at my home, mostly. I've got to be where I can be reached."

Chapter 16

It had been a disappointing, sometimes maddening three weeks since Tracy left the valley of Bear Creek and worked his patient way onto the desert. The first frustration had come when he reached the cow camp of Ridge Durnbo. There he had learned from an Indian with a small command of English that Durnbo had lost nearly all his cattle in the winter blizzard. Undaunted, he and his partner had gone to the Umpqua, where they now were, to buy more. The Indian camp tender had no idea when they would be back. Nor had he seen any activity by other white men in that vicinity, recently or — except for the emigrant wagons — the summer before.

It was a vast, lonely and lethal desert, and while Tracy admired Durnbo's determination, he marveled at his audacity. This region was part of the great lava plateau formed when Mount Shasta spewed molten rock hundreds of miles to the east. Thinly soiled even yet, it grew the bunchgrass Durnbo utilized, but beyond that little more than sage and rabbit brush and thin patches of juniper trees. Even the Indians who roamed it to hunt and prey confined their habitations to the few watered and sheltered valleys. From Tracy's viewpoint, it presented not a dearth but a defeating multitude of places in which what he must find could be hidden.

Denied such help as the cowman might have given him, Tracy had turned his attention to another lead that had been opened at Camp Baker, the night he took Nan there for safekeeping. It was his first meeting with Lindsay Applegate, who commanded the Baker Guards, the company that had ridden escort on the previous season's wagon trains and who knew the emigrant road in detail.

"Colonel Ross's kept me up on what's going on," Applegate said, that night. "I've given it thought and questioned the boys. None of us can recall a blamed thing to suggest guns were smuggled over our section of the road, let alone cached along it somewhere. The last sign of them was there at the burned wagon, on east of our reach of the road."

"Nan wasn't trying to mislead me," Tracy said stubbornly. She had already been given quarters, and he was alone with the captain. "If she had been, Hackett wouldn't have blown up like he did."

"I've known Nan a long time," Applegate agreed. "She might do something foolish if she was in love, but she's a good woman. And now that she's made me think of it it could be those guns never came our way at all. You been in the Great Bend?"

"Of the Humboldt? No."

"It's this side of where they found the burned wagons. But the other side of where the settlers turn off to come our way. Most of the ones going to California go on down the Humboldt, and there's a branch they can take that runs east of the Humboldt Mountains. There's some mining camps in there."

"I've heard of them. Star City, Dixie and a couple of others." Tracy paused, musing. "Dixie? Whoever named that camp had Southern sentiments."

Applegate grinned. "And right above it's Unionville. You'd think the two camps were fighting the war right there."

"It's not very convenient to the area we think Tremaine plans to take over."

"No, but it sets at the forks of the roads that lead into it."

So, having failed to connect with Durnbo, Tracy had come on to Star City, presently the largest of the eastern camps. At first he had been encouraged by what he found. Like the Comstock, to the south, this was a silver camp, boasting a population of about twelve hundred, with a few good mines like the Sheba and DeSoto, and a hundred lesser mines and worthless prospects. It was important enough, he was surprised to learn, that a special telegraph line had been built from Virginia City, and this increased his interest. Tremaine had no known investment here, but that did not preclude secret connections, while the telegraph gave swift communication with known parts of the apparatus.

It had all come to naught. By day Tracy had poked around mines and prospects all along the eastern slope of the Humboldts, less hopeful of making a discovery than of arousing counter-action that might open a lead. The evenings he spent in saloons, gambling houses and dead-falls, his ears open but hearing nothing helpful. So he had written it off as another blind alley, finally. Now he was nearing Tule Lake again, on his way back to Jacksonville but meaning to check again at Durnbo's camp.

The lake covered miles of the floor of a vast depression in the desert. Islands stood offshore in the slack runoff of Lost River, which had pooled and evaporated here for countless ages. Tules fringed the banks, and along the far and southern shore lay scabby crusts of lava. Tracy followed the emigrant road down to the narrow east shore and turned north. The hoofs of the bay pounded their prints into those of thousands of mules, horses and oxen and of dried and groaning wheels.

A point thrust out at the north end of this shore, pinching the road against the tules. Beyond it was a flat of wild ryegrass that spring had started growing, and the site showed signs of many a wagon camp. At the corner of the lake, Lost River came into the tules, flowing strongly now but a trickle in summer. The road turned up the river and in a few miles forded the stream and struck west. Familiar with the vicinity now, Tracy kept on along an Indian trail, coming presently into widening beautiful country that Ridge Durnbo had appropriated.

Suddenly Tracy smiled. Ahead of him, and off across the gentle, juniper-dotted slopes, grazed cattle. Durnbo was back. He lifted the speed of the horse and, just at sundown, came to the dugout where the cowman lived with his partner.

By the time he rode up, Durnbo had

climbed to the top of the steps. The curiosity left the man's face, giving way to a broad grin. "Look who's here!" he said heartily. "Did you finally come out for some deer hunting?"

"Just for a hunt." Tracy swung down.

They shook hands, and Tracy looked around, liking what he saw, primitive and austere as it was. Almost any way he looked, he could see steers. The horses used on the drive, but not of immediate need, were mixed with the cattle. He turned back to see another man come up the steps.

"Shake hands with my pardner, Jim Rivers," Durnbo said. "This is Tracy Dalton, Jim. The fella that kept me from getting a knife between my ribs in J'Ville. I asked him to come out and hunt antelope, and here he is, finally."

"You're only partly correct," Tracy said. "I'm hunting rebels."

They thought he was joking until he explained his true identity and mission.

Rivers was a small, wiry man, but the fact that he was out here on an Indian-infested desert with Durnbo proved he was cut from the same bolt of cloth. But neither man had any more to tell Tracy than he had learned from the Indian camp tender on his first visit. Nonetheless they insisted on his spending the night with them.

They had finished supper in the warm, lantern-lit dugout when Durnbo stared suddenly at his partner and said, "Jim, how about the lava beds?"

"Could be," Rivers answered. "But any man that'd winter in there'd have to want his hide damned bad."

"What beds do you mean?" Tracy asked.

Durnbo laughed. "The ones south of the lake. They're mighty big, mebbe twelve miles each way. What Jim meant is that they look like hell turned wrongside out, when you're in 'em. I ain't been there in ages. You, Jim?"

Rivers shook his head. "Nope. Accordin' to Cultus Charlie, the Injuns don't go in anymore, either. He says they've been haunted lately."

"Haunted?" Tracy exclaimed. "And they're close to the emigrant road, too, aren't they?"

"Touch it," Durnbo said, "where it reaches the lake." Tracy said energetically, "By golly. Maybe those haunts are fakes to keep the Indians away from there."

Durnbo scratched his thick thatch, his eyes gleaming. "Maybe you had the right pew but the wrong church when you went over to Star City. There's the same split in the emigrant trail there on the south end of the lake. Likely you didn't notice it. The south branch ain't used by wagons or even much by emigrants. Folks in a rush to get between J'Ville and Virginia City travel it horseback. And, by damn, Hackett's used it with his packstrings."

"There's sure to be caves in those beds," Tracy mused. "You can count on that, any place there's lava rock." Durnbo was grinning broadly. "What say you and me take a little look down there tomorrow?"

"That," Tracy said, "will more than square anything you think you owe me, whether or not we turn up anything. But I've got a feeling."

"I got one like it."

Tracy had been let down too many times to grow overly excited, but the sign was right, at last. Wagons regularly fell behind the trains they traveled with, to make repairs, rest the draft animals or just to rest the people. If the insurrectionists' gun cache was a cave in the lavas, the Indian belief in recent haunts meant a guard had been left there. So it would have been simple for a wagon, or many of them, to drop off contraband that could be picked up by pack animals and taken to the cache. From this region ran trails to every part of the endangered country, and Hack Hackett often passed the spot.

Durnbo took Tracy out on a new route, the next morning, saying the best way to approach a haunted lava bed was gingerly. Instead of following down Lost River to the lake, they crossed at the upstream emigrant ford and for a time rode west. Durnbo not only wore a sidearm, he had a carbine booted to the saddle. They rode unhurriedly, as if heading for Jacksonville, until, wordlessly, Durnbo finally cut south from the trail.

They entered a region of crowded hills and fractured plateaus whose roughness explained why the cattlemen had not often visited the vicinity. Yet Durnbo had a knack with such country and kept them moving at a pace that put the miles behind. When the sun marked noon, they ate cold biscuits from the saddlebags without stopping. Two hours thereafter, they pulled up on a bluff that looked out on a scene of astonishing wilderness.

Tracy saw that they were now south of the big lake, and what he now discerned below them was like a stormy sea that somehow had been petrified. There was nothing but this jagged rock, which seemed devoid of life until he noticed, here and there, puny patches of sage or bunchgrass that had gained a footing in some dusting of soil.

"If they've got a camp in there," Durnbo said quietly, "it's likely in reach of the lake. Not much as drinkin' water, but all there is after the rain that collects in the pools dries up."

Tracy nodded. "If we can follow the shore, we might find their sign. But look, my friend. I can't ask you to go in there with me."

"If you thought you had to ask me, I'd bust your jaw." Durnbo glanced around. "The first thing's to get down there."

That proved fairly easy, a little farther on where the bluff broke into terraces and slants they could follow down. Between the rim and where the rock fields began in earnest was an open strip that let them ride to the lake shore. Yet it was immediately apparent that this was as far as they could go with horses. Durnbo looked at the sun and grunted, "We'll eat a late supper, tonight." They watered the animals in a natural cistern, then left them in the brush and went on along the shore, Durnbo carrying the carbine.

For about a mile they moved due east, then a rocky point shoved itself deep into the lake ahead. So far they had come upon no evidence of other visitors, or life of any sort. They found they could get around the point and were spared the hard, dangerous job of trying to climb over it. On the far side they came upon what clearly was an old Indian trail, scuffed by moccasins but not used in quite a while.

"Comes in from the wagon road side," Durnbo commented. "And if Injuns can get in here from there, so can your Johnny Rebs."

Excitement and a genuine hope of accomplishment had started to build in Tracy. He nodded, saying nothing. Craggy, sawtooth outcrops rose ahead of them, bulking into the sky. The air off the lake was cool and rank.

Just under the crags they came upon a sight that stopped them still. A heavily used, fresh trail came in from the other direction, turned in and vanished into a narrow fissure in the jagged upthrusts.

"Horses aplenty," Durnbo breathed. "Or mules. No Injun ever shoed his pony, even if they had reason to bring so many into this God-forsaken place. Old son, we've treed your coon."

Tracy was sure of that and also that from there on they would be in mortally dangerous territory. If this was the cache, it was more than well located for Tremaine's purpose. In terrain like this, a small force could hold it against a huge one.

"One thing's sure," he answered. "It's got to be investigated. And if it's what we think, it's going to take Applegate's company, at least, to storm it. Now, don't give me an argument. I want you to go to Camp Baker, tell them what we've found and that we need help with it. Meanwhile, I'll try to get the lay of the land."

"But —" Durnbo began, then he broke off, nodding. "You're right. But I hate to leave you here on your lonesome."

"It's my job. You get going, and take my horse. It would be a dead giveaway if it was found where it is."

Durnbo insisted on his taking the carbine, transferred a pocketful of shells, then slipped away and soon vanished. Tracy lingered a few moments, studying the local detail. Tracks at the edge of the lake showed this was where the renegades watered their animals and got at least part of the water for their own use. Some of the tracks were fresh, but no large body had come in or gone out in the last few days.

He went on carefully, moving to the fissure that let the train run deeper into the lava beds.

The passage was wider than it had looked from a distance, and toothlike pinnacles abutted it on either side. He couldn't guess how far it wormed its way into the awesome region, although it bent out of sight about a hundred yards ahead. At this point there was no way to climb to a higher elevation and skirt the trail in greater safety. He started in along the floor.

The first dogleg only opened into another. Tracy had no idea why he did not stumble into a sentry, unless the long, untroubled sojourn here had made the occupants overly confident. He covered about half a mile and was still probing his way into what Durnbo had aptly called hell turned inside out. He even thought he could smell smoke. Then, in relief, he came to a place where he could climb from the fissure bottom. His footing thereafter was precarious, but he felt safer, and doubly careful of making a betraying noise, went on until again he stopped in wonder.

Ahead yawned a crater that could have swallowed half a city block. The smell of smoke had not been imagined, and now he saw its source. All around the walls of the sunken pit were grottos, caverns and fissures that had been turned into human habitations. This much he took in with a glance, then he ducked back, not daring to expose himself too long. But he knew he had reached his goal and he was not encouraged by its formidable aspect. He crawled for some distance to his right, then bellied in for another look at the place.

The smoke came from a fire in the center of this natural and hidden village. Half a dozen men were stretched about it, smoking and drinking coffee. He could see others lying on bedrolls in the cavern across from him. Another cave was piled with stores, and he knew that in yet another were the guns he had sought so long.

Withdrawing again, he lay on the sharp rock, blood pounding in his lungs and head. Tremaine and Hackett had made this cache last fall, not only because boxed guns were a cumbersome item to smuggle into crowded areas. By keeping the ammunition and firearms separated, they stood to minimize the loss should the authorities decide to make a legal search of one of the suspected mines. The two items would not be brought together until the last moment, which was due or overdue already. Hackett would do the final transportation, shooting his way to the rebel units if necessary. He would have to bring in the animals, since the force here seemed to have none, unless they were kept in some hidden valley where there was water and grass.

It was not wise to remain this close to the hideout, and Tracy wanted to learn something of the trail that led from here to the emigrant road. He felt confident of Applegate's prompt appearance, once he had been informed of the situation. Before his arrival, Tracy hoped to figure out a way to assault the stronghold that would not cost too heavily in life.

Rising, he retraced his steps and let himself down into the jagged, wall-girt trail that ran the three-quarters of a mile to the lake. He did not draw a full breath until he was out of the passage, in which he would be hopelessly trapped if somebody happened along. Pressed into the shoreside brush, presently, he rested. He was all too aware that he had crowded his luck to the limit and beyond, that he had a long time to survive out here before help could arrive.

The area was already in shadow because the lowering sun was cut off by the uprises. He decided to stay where he was until after dark, then make his way to the emigrant road. He moved down and got a drink, finding the water drinkable but unpleasant. Then he went farther back along the old Indian trail to await the night.

Just before dark a man came out of the cleft, not a hundred yards from where Tracy was hidden. A Chinese yoke laid across his shoulders, and from it dangled two large wooden pails. He went down to the water's edge and filled the containers, but before shouldering the load stuffed and lighted his pipe. He stood for several minutes looking out over the twilit lake, then he hoisted the yoke and vanished into the badlands.

Tracy waited for another hour, then emerged and started east along the shore. Several points ran into the lake, but the trail surmounted them easily and was not hard to follow even in the night. All along, the lava field crowded close to the water. He had gone about as far as he had come with Durnbo from the other direction when he reached what seemed to be a peninsular outthrust. The trail climbed directly over it through narrow jaws of sheer rock. The rise was slight, and he quickly topped it to be swallowed by the rock.

At that precise instant he tripped and

sprawled headlong, the wall-swelled crack of a rifle splitting the night and beating his ears.

He landed hard, taking skin from his elbows on the jagged rock, his eardrums buzzing. He tried to shake the confusion from his brain and scramble to his feet, uncertain if he should go forward or back. They had stretched a rope across the trail, he realized, rigged to a rifle whose firing would warn them of a prowler coming in from the road at night. He didn't know if it was near enough to the stronghold for the sound to be heard there. Perhaps it would carry, with so much rock to resound it. But it was more likely that there were men hereabouts.

He hadn't passed any men to be aware of them, but turning back would keep him in restricted quarters. Grasping his gun, he ran forward. Shouts sounded on his left, and he realized they had a camp on the peninsula, right at hand, fireless because the light could be seen from across the lake or from the road. The cries were pitching back and forth, so there were several men after him already. He halted for a second, realizing that the lava field fell back abruptly on this side of the gut. He cut off the trail, making his way to the right, away from the yelling.

A shout that sounded right behind him punched into his still ringing ears.

"Stop in your tracks, or you're dead!"

He was too far from cover to keep going with anything but suicidal results. He swung to fight for it, but even as he turned he saw other men appear on the trail not forty feet away, their firearms covering him. He let his gun drop and lifted his hands.

"It's the galoot Hack sent word about," one of them said. "The army gumshoe. Dalton."

Chapter 17

Lorna sat with her sewing, having no interest in adding a stitch to the housedress she had been making. But she was in desperate need of something to which she could rivet her mind. Alan sat across the fireplace from her, smoking a cigar while he watched the flames, absorbed in his secret thoughts. After storming out of the house, the night before, and being gone all day, he had come home at suppertime as if nothing was wrong between them at all.

Yet she could guess the nature of his thoughts, for she knew he had set dreadful events in motion while he was gone. Now he sat like a general at a command post, waiting for his orders to be translated into achievements that would glorify him. He was forcing her to accept it, to be as criminal as he was through her silence, because she had loved and married him. But he no longer tried to corrupt her with his talk of power and wealth and greatness.

She was not sure what fetters caused her to accept his will. She was too stunned, disillusioned and angry to decide if she still loved him. But there were other shackles. She was his wife and at this moment, without having discovered it, could be carrying his child. There was nothing she could think of to do that would make her less miserable, even if it might ease her conscience. Under these circumstances was the basic fact that she could do nothing that might result in the death with which he so recklessly flirted.

The emotional drain had wearied her, but she made herself keep sewing until the mantle clock struck ten and she could put down the material. Alan looked up when finally she rose from her chair.

"Going to bed so early?" he said.

She nodded and went out.

She did not like sharing a bedroom under conditions like these. It was like sleeping with a wholly strange man because it could not be avoided, a helpless, hopeless kind of whoring. She undressed quickly, blew out the light and slipped into bed. Mercifully he did not follow to try to soften her with lovemaking. She had dozed off when she felt his weight settle in the bed, and she did not know how much later it was. He didn't approach her.

Nor did she know how deep in the night

it was when a loud thumping awakened her. Alan shoved up on his arms, and she saw him glance down at her. She didn't stir. He slid out of bed, catching his robe off the foot and donning it as he went out. The knocks came again, urgently. It was at the front door. Alan closed the bedroom door when he left the room.

She slipped out of bed then, and moved over to the door in her bare feet. She heard the front door open, and Alan said, his voice grown tense, "What brings you here, Jake? Is something wrong out there?"

"Mebbe so, mebbe not," a man's voice answered.

She had no idea who Jake could be. The men were silent, and she heard the outer door close. Then light flickered and steadied under the bedroom door, and she knew Alan had lighted a lamp. He said, "Keep your voice down. My wife's sleeping in the next room."

Lorna could still hear, although Jake lowered his voice obediently. "Hackett says for you to send him every man you can raise. Pronto."

"To the lava beds?" Alan said sharply. "What for?"

"We caught the army feller. Dalton. He'd been in to the cache. He knows everything now. That was early in the evening, and Hack got in with the mule string around midnight. On the way he caught a feller heading for J'Ville. That Durnbo that runs cattle on the Lost. He was leadin' that bay of Dalton's. Hack recognized it. Durnbo denied knowing anything about Dalton, but Hack knew better. He's got 'em both there at the cache, but he wants more help and fast."

"Why?" Alan said.

"Maybe there was men with 'em we didn't catch. That pair won't say. If there was more, the militia could land on us afore we get them guns away."

"It's five o'clock," Alan said worriedly. "It'll be daylight in another hour. You go on to Gold Hill, Jake. Tell Bide not to leave the mine unguarded, but to let you have every man he can scare up horses for."

"Hack said for me to get back on the double."

"I'll go out to the desert. This time Dalton'll tell me what I want to know or die on the spot."

There was no more talking. Lorna heard the door close again and hurried back to bed. Through slitted eyelids, she saw Alan come into the bedroom, highlighted by the lamp in the parlor. She didn't move while his gaze rested on her briefly. Then he began to dress in the rough clothes he wore when he rode. He got his revolver out of the bureau drawer and carried it into the other room, shutting the door behind him.

She lay with her heart thudding. She had just heard him threaten to kill Tracy, at least to torture him into making him talk. She wondered how many men had already died because they had got in Alan's way. Her mind recoiled against considering those who would die, now that he was pushing his plans to completion.

Fate had not done enough to her when it disclosed as a traitor the man she had married and followed across the continent. It had gone on to place Alan in the balance with Tracy, whose life she might yet save if she could bring herself to betray Alan. It was too vast and too cruel a quandary. All she could do was lie helplessly, her stomach filled with sickness.

She heard him leave the house and got up and went into the parlor. It was cold and dark, for he had extinguished the light, and the fire had long since burned out. Her sewing lay folded on the table, where she had left it. Beside it was Alan's humidor of cigars.

Abruptly she was back at the church where they were married, coming down the steps between masses of relatives, friends and neighbors, who were showering them with rice. She remembered the red line on his jaw where he had, in his nervousness, cut himself that morning while shaving.

The darkness past the window was thinning. She went back to the bedroom and dressed, donning a blouse, her riding skirt and boots. At the Arkansas stable, ten minutes later, she asked for a saddlehorse.

Chapter 18

Long before Hackett's mule train reached the lavas, Tracy had known that nothing but his own nimble wits had kept him alive. His captors had been about to take him into the stronghold where, if he was not shot summarily, his chance of escape would be nil. Even while standing on the lakeshore trail under their menacing guns, he had seen the need to confuse them to the utmost.

"Careful, boys!" he shouted, as if to someone in the benighted distance. "They've got a trap!"

The men who had converged on him so menacingly looked around in quick uneasiness.

"Which way'd you come from, Dalton?" one of them demanded.

Tracy had not been sure until then that, to avoid dreary vigils, they had relied on their signal and had not seen him until after the rifle went off. If he could make them think he had not discovered the stronghold and had help of his own in the area, they might keep him out here where the terrain was less difficult to move in.

"He's only tryin' to run a sandy," another man scoffed. "He's a lone wolf, and there ain't anybody else but us."

"It's been a while since they sent word he was racking around out here," the first said uncertainly. "Where've you been the last two-three weeks, Dalton? Since you lit out of J'Ville?"

"Here and there," Tracy said. "Or, if you prefer, to and fro."

"You been down to Fort Churchill?"

"Maybe I'm just a desert fancier," Tracy laughed. "Making nature studies. You do run into weird specimens out here."

His questioner said annoyedly, "Take him over to our camp, boys. I'll go in and ask Jake Sprague what to do with him."

The guards' cold camp was on the blind side of the big sentinel rocks, hidden in a nest of lava. Three men took Tracy there, while the others stayed out on the trail, no longer sure they were masters of the situation. After a time Jake Sprague arrived, the man who seemed to boss the bunch in the lava beds. Sprague had had no success, himself, in wringing from Tracy any assurance that he did not have confederates, somewhere out in the night.

The stratagem had bought Tracy time,

and then, around midnight, Hackett had arrived with Ridge Durnbo his captive. Tracy's heart sank, at that, for Durnbo's bad luck ended all hope of help from Camp Baker. Yet it demonstrated that his own bluff about others around had been the best move of his life. Hackett had insisted on strong reinforcements before he attempted to move the guns, and Sprague had departed posthaste for Jacksonville.

Afterward Hackett had taken his big mule train on into the lavas, leaving Durnbo and Tracy at the outpost, tied hand and foot with rawhide strips and under the eye of a mean-looking guard. Sprague had brought men from the stronghold and posted a bristling defense at the point where Tracy had met his downfall.

"Come daylight, and we can see to track," Hackett had said angrily to Tracy, "we'll see about your supposed amigos."

Now only an hour or two of the night remained. Daylight was sure to disclose how the stronghold had been approached and by how many men. If he and Durnbo were to have a chance, Tracy realized, it had to come very soon.

The men who had manned this outpost since the fall before had done what they could to make it comfortable. Broken rock surrounded it, and a brush and canvas shelter had been put up to protect the guards from the elements. Apparently they went up to the stronghold in relays for their meals. They could not have the comfort of a fire and hot coffee, but bedding showed that they slept here.

Tracy sat with his numb legs thrust straight out, his aching back against a rock. Durnbo was on his right. The guard had forbidden talking, and Tracy didn't yet know how Durnbo had fallen into Hackett's hands. The guard was seated some twenty feet from them and watched them steadily. He had a rifle across his lap.

In sudden annoyance, Durnbo said, "Hey, Johnny Reb. Any reason why a man can't have a drink of water?"

The guard pondered that a moment, then rose and walked over to the shelter to get a canteen that hung on an upright.

"They caught me just when I reached the emigrant road," Durnbo whispered to Tracy. "Your horse spilled everything."

"Rotten luck. Any chance of your partner showing up here?"

Durnbo shook his head. "He won't even worry till it's too late. I'm gone overnight lots."

"We've got till daylight. Maybe an hour or two, afterward."

The guard was coming back. He refused to come close enough to hand over the canteen, instead tossing it at Durnbo's feet.

"How's a hog-tied man gonna get the cap off of that thing?" Durnbo demanded.

"It's your thirst," the guard said and laughed. "So that's your worry, buck."

They were a vicious lot which, Tracy reflected, seemed a good estimate of Tremaine's whole crew. Not a man of them had a whit of interest in the Confederate cause. They were out for themselves. He was quite sure that also was true of Alan Tremaine.

Durnbo tried to work the canteen in closer but only succeeded in pushing it closer to Tracy than to himself. Tracy swung on his haunches and found he could hook his heels over it. He worked it in to him, pulling it under the fold of his knees. Spreading the knees as far as his lashed ankles would allow, he tried to bend forward far enough to catch the chain that fastened the cap to the canteen with his teeth. He couldn't quite do it.

The guard chuckled. "Back a little stiff, Dalton? Mebbe I ought to limber it up with snake oil."

"You belong in a medicine show, all right," Durnbo snorted. "You're so danged comical."

Tracy used his heels to work the canteen back farther, his clumsy attempts only amusing the guard. But when he bent down again, he caught the chain in his teeth and slowly raised the container upright. By clamping it between his knees, he was able to loosen and then work off the cap with his teeth.

"Now, how're you gonna drink it?" the guard jeered. "Want I should find you a grass straw?"

Tracy let his awkward efforts tip over the canteen. He made a despairing shrug with his shoulders, and the water gurgled out to pool in a depression on the rock floor at his feet.

"Too bad," the guard sympathized. "But if you're only gonna spill it, I'm damned if I'll tote you more."

Durnbo was quiet, for he had grasped Tracy's intention, which the guard so far had not. When wet, rawhide had a capacity to stretch considerably. Tracy had shoved his legs straight angrily, seeming to give up, but the lower part of his ankle bindings was immersed in the pooled water. Still smiling over his tormenting trick, the guard began to roll a cigarette.

Tracy let the water soften the raw leather for a long while, watching the darkness give way to growing light. When finally he changed position, he kept a leg thrust stiffly straight and drew back hard on the other. The thong slipped upward on the boottop of the stiffened leg. As if settling himself more comfortably, he reversed the procedure, and the binding loosed a little more. But the knot only drew tighter, and the leather hadn't stretched enough to let him work one foot through.

He noticed that the guard was watching him and rested until the hard case looked away. Then he buckled his knees, drawing his heels up to his thighs. With his boottops protecting his shins, he could stand a lot of pressure, and he exerted his full strength trying to force his knees apart. The purchase was very poor in that position. But the wet rawhide was loose on his ankles, and the exertions were restoring circulation to his cramped legs. Canting a foot so the toes dug against the rock, he tried straightening the opposite leg. He had much more purchase that way. He brought his weight farther forward to increase the drag and keep the obstructed foot from moving. He could hear blood crash in his ears when, with all his strength, he forced the other leg outward a few inches. The rawhide had stretched some more.

He still felt like a fly caught in molasses, but his determination only mounted. He pushed his right leg through the loops nearly to the top of his boot, the curve of the ankle and calf acting as a wedge. The guard still had not caught on. When Tracy worked the rawhide down loose on the ankle, he thought he had a chance to work one foot out and free.

Durnbo did not seem to be paying attention, but he had followed every movement. Knowing the next effort had to be a reckless gamble, he called wheedlingly to the guard.

"All right, mister, you had your fun. Now how about givin' us a drink? Me, I ain't had water since yesterday."

The man laughed but less maliciously. "Learned to be polite, did you?"

He had no intention of complying, but he was giving his attention to Durnbo, which was all Tracy needed. Moving a foot until he had hooked a bootheel on the binding, Tracy quietly worked the other foot free.

Staring on past the guard, then, Tracy

let a look of excitement form on his face while he shouted, "Come on, boys! There's only one of 'em here!"

Worry jerked the guard around, swinging the rifle to cover his rear. As he turned, Tracy drove forward with a raised shoulder and bent head, his back bowed. The thudding impact stopped the man before he could cry out a warning to his fellows, turning the sound into a sickened gush of air. Momentum drove him backward, spilling him in a free fall. Tracy went with him, but the fellow's body softened the jar, although his bound hands gave him no chance to protect himself otherwise. He rolled heels over head and came to rest on his back, momentarily stunned. His vision was blurry when he forced himself to get up, but the guard didn't stir at all.

Staggering to the water bucket on a box in the shelter, Tracy backed up to it. Then he bent his knees until his wrist bindings were submerged, his eyes watching toward the trail. But the guard hadn't had time to call for help, and the short fracas had made little noise. The danger was from someone straying in. Yet he had to stand there, his awkwardly bent knees beginning to tremble, long enough for the rawhide to soften.

When finally he made the effort, there was no leather boottop to protect the flesh of his wrists. Yet he wrenched and twisted them savagely, and by the time he brought his hands up free, the tissue was torn and bleeding.

Durnbo had watched hypnotically, not uttering a sound. Tracy freed him and let Durnbo work off his stiffness while he hunted up a box of extra shells for the guard's rifle. Then, taking the rifle, they slipped away on the opposite side of the camp from the trail. This would take them onto the peninsula that ran into the lake, but Tracy wanted distance primarily. Afterward they could work down to the shore and try to get out to the emigrant road. If that was not possible, they would move west along the old trail they had first followed into the lava beds.

A half hour later they were down on the lake, and there had been no outcry behind them. But even if they were not missed at once Hackett would soon have parties out searching for Tracy's possible confederates. Durnbo said, "Sure wish we could get a couple of their cayuses."

"So do I, but it's too dangerous. We've got to walk to your cow camp, then I'll go to Camp Baker as fast as one of your horses will carry me."

"They'll have help from the Lady Luck and be gone before you could make it. I heard a couple of 'em talkin' while they were bringing me back. Sibley got his tail feathers pulled. That's all I heard, except that he lost his supplies."

"My God," Tracy breathed. "And Tremaine's fool enough to go ahead on his own."

"Seems to have made him all the more determined."

"He's a mad dog. They all are. We've got to stop them."

"I allow as to that," Durnbo agreed. "My only puzzlement is what with."

They walked steadily along the lake shore, finding that the trail was south of it some distance. It, too, seemed deserted, for they heard nothing. Presently they reached the southeastern corner of the lake. They were almost past the lavas, for the country to the south was more open. But Hackett and twenty or thirty others must be scouring the country by now. The tracks of the fugitives were bound to be discovered and followed. Now that he knew they were dealing with utterly desperate men, Tracy was deeply worried.

He explained the bluff he had run about

others being in earshot when he was captured, which had stalled Hackett and caused him to send to Tremaine for additional men. "They'll see through that, pretty soon," he concluded. "Then Hackett's going to load his mule train and travel. How far are we from your camp?"

"Twenty-thirty miles."

"You were right. We can't reach it, ride to Jacksonville and get back with help before late tomorrow. Hackett's going out of here with those guns long before then. He'll cut up the train and send part to each of their ammunition caches. That far ahead of us, and scattered, they can't help but beat us."

Calmly, Durnbo said, "If you're goin' back, so'm I. Don't call it patriotism. I don't know what a man owes his country. I do know about a man and his friend. I know what you're thinkin', too. If we could hold that portal they've got to come through with their mules, we might pin 'em there in the malpais a long while. Wonder if Hackett took off the guards there to help hunt for us?"

"It's worth finding out."

"So let's find out."

In spite of their long, roundabout walk, Tracy knew they had not moved eastward more than a couple of miles. Hackett would have thrown every available man into the hunt, but it was not the guard outpost that Tracy had in mind. The narrow, rock-walled canyon of nearly a mile that connected the stronghold with the lake edge was the renegades' weakness. They had no guards there, instead had relied on the outpost for security. One man with a rifle on top of that canyon could close and keep it closed as long as his ammunition lasted. It had to be tried before Hackett got out with his loaded mules, and there was no denying that it was an all but suicidal undertaking.

"Thanks, my friend," he said gently. "But it'll be no good unless there's help on the way. You've got to go on. That's dangerous enough, since I'll have to take our only weapon."

"Now, look —" Durnbo protested.

"We had this out once before."

Durnbo nodded. Then he offered his hand, turned and walked on, while Tracy went to the right, toward the trail leading back into the lavas.

He stuck with the trail only a few minutes, then crossed it and pressed on into cover on the south side. Daylight was strong now, a clear, cool morning under a nearly empty desert sky. The lavas broke to the west like solidified surf, scabrous scars inflicted in bygone ages upon a tortured earth. He kept hidden from the trail, but no sound came from it. Then he was on the rubbled plain and slanting slowly toward the first low, jagged peaks. He had no idea of what difficulties lay between him and the point of vantage he hoped to reach.

Presently he had the impression of looking upon the dead craters of the moon. Yet, so far, the going was less difficult than he had expected. He was slowed by having to pick his way, angling around fissures and walls, sometimes retreating to try another way. Needles, cones and pits lay all about him. Frequently the rock under his feet rang with a hollow sound. Here and there a grubby sage brush had found a foothold in thin soil. An occasional magpie slashed across the morning light.

It was hard to measure distance, but Tracy tried to keep close to the lake so as to strike the canyon he had in mind. He was warned that he was near, presently, by the two sawtooths that marked the entrance to the stronghold. A few minutes later he had reached them and halted at a spot on the western face of the near one.

At the moment there was no one in the chiseled trench that was Hackett's only exit from the contraband cache.

Tracy prepared his position carefully, piling trash rock to make a breastwork through whose opening he could see nearly all the canyon. The sawtooth protected his rear, and he was exposed only from across the gap. He opened the box of shells and placed them handily, checked the rifle, then settled down to wait.

The first sign of life came from the lake side in about an hour. Tracy heard the strike of hoofs on rock well before three riders appeared from the right, going into the stronghold. He let them pass unmolested, for the more of them he could catch inside the better his chances. They disappeared at the upper end of the slot, where it turned. And all the movement for the next hour was in that direction. The renegades were giving up the search, probably with the idea of pulling out with the guns as swiftly as they could. For another long period, the passage was empty.

He had not eaten in twenty-four hours, and then only a couple of biscuits. He had not slept in a greater time and since had asked much of his body. Yet he felt nothing beyond the hard set of muscle and an acuteness of sense he had never experienced before.

Then his ears caught the sound of massed hoofs. They were coming out with the mule train.

He had range to command all the canyon he could see, and he had his plan worked out. First to appear was a horse and rider, the latter not Hackett but a mulero riding point to coax the animals to follow. The first mule came out of the jog, under pack, its load covered with a tarpaulin. Tracy's finger tightened on the trigger, but still he waited. Mule by mule they appeared, stringing toward him. He counted ten, then another ten, and his finger itched to function. Yet he still waited, for he knew Hackett had fifty or more mules with him.

When half of them were in sight, Tracy opened fire, the crash of his rifle splitting the silence and bouncing on a thousand rock surfaces. His second shot punched after it, a third, and on until he had emptied the rifle. He ignored the one visible rider, whose horse was rearing and wheeling, and aimed at the mules on which Hackett's mobility depended. If he could put enough of them out of business, he might delay things until he could get help.

The three mules in the lead had gone down, he saw. Those behind piled on them, their braying shaking the canyon. Two or three more crumpled more slowly but were hit and going down.

He reloaded swiftly. When he looked again the rider was flogging the milling animals, his shouts replacing the percussion of shots. He was trying to harry the unharmed mules back into cover and get out of harm's way, himself. Tracy began to shoot again, a distasteful duty imposed by his need to save a greater number of human lives. More of them dropped, dotting the canyon floor up there. But now other riders were forcing their way through into view. They seemed to have gotten the train straightened out beyond the jog. Now they were quirting and cursing the visible animals still on their feet, trying to move them back out of sight.

The rifle went empty again. By the time Tracy reloaded, there was nothing on the canyon floor but unmoving muscle that would never transport traitors' guns. His ears rang from the shooting, and the gun barrel was hot. Its smell and that of hanging powder smoke reeked in his nose. Again he was alone with emptiness and loneliness and the knowledge that he had destroyed a worthwhile part of Hackett's available transportation.

They knew by now that they had no chance to get out with more than a remnant, if that much, of the train. Unless they removed him, and that would be their next objective. Somehow he had to make that cost them time, too, a lot of it.

For what seemed ages there was no sign of movement on their part at all. Tracy knew this could be a fatal impression. To destroy him, they would have to come on top the beds themselves. Knowing this was how it would be, he had selected the highest position possible, except for the sawtooth across the canyon. He could do nothing but watch that. The whole near side was smooth, and nobody could come over the top without his knowing it. But he could not look in all directions at once . . .

The sun stood at high noon, and he had begun to worry. Perhaps there was another way out of the stronghold he had not discovered, which they had taken with what was left of the train. He dismissed an uneasy impulse to move closer and check. They would have tried to salvage at least some of the guns still up there on the canyon floor, transferring some to their saddle horses, loading the remaining mules more heavily.

All at once he was wholly attentive to his surroundings. A rock had rolled somewhere, the faintest jar in the air. As his eyes darted about, a rifle crashed, and a bullet spanged off a rock next to him. A daub of smoke on the opposite side told him that one or more of them had got in over there. He fired to let them know he had them located and hold them down, seeing chips fly off the ridge-line rock. A glance up the canyon showed him men boiling into view. He understood it. They meant to strip the dead mules of packs and saddles while the men on the other sawtooth diverted, if they could not kill him.

He fired two shots at the group on the floor, only to be shot at twice from across the way. There were at least two of them up here. He fired again in their direction. The men in the canyon swarmed like ants over the downed mules and their packs. Tracy could not stop them, for a third man soon joined the line across. They were high enough even to nullify his shallow breastworks. He had to give them his full attention. And by the same means, he understood, they would try to run their renovated pack train down the canyon and from under the menace he posed.

The men across seemed to be waiting on that big rush before they exposed themselves again to shoot. Tracy built up his rifle pit with what rubble he could reach or rake in with a foot. After that came another nerve-straining wait.

Then sound rent the air again, and his body jerked as if it had been harpooned. All he felt was the impact, then numbness all through his side. The left side — and this awareness cleared his brain somewhat. He turned his head and there on the south side of the outcrop above him stood Hack Hackett, raised up to get a better shot at him.

Tracy realized they had opened up from across the canyon, also, trying to draw his attention away from Hackett. He swung the rifle just as Hackett shot. A bullet kicked cinders in his face, and he clawed his eyes free to see Hackett stagger sidewise and lose his footing. Then the packer slid down to the lip of the canyon and went over. His body turned slowly in the air as it fell.

There was a cry of concern from across the canyon. Bullets from there peppered his flimsy fortification. Tracy's groggy mind tried to cope with it, and from the corner of his eye he saw pack animals, filing into view in the canyon. They didn't need Hackett, for this was Alan Tremaine's undertaking. With a groan he shifted the rifle and emptied it into the canyon. The pack animals came on. His fingers were numb and clumsy when he tried to reload. It seemed to take him a long while, and bullets kept raining against the rocks about him. That didn't matter. He had to stop the mule train.

When he looked into the canyon again, the last of the train had vanished beneath him.

He had failed.

He realized that the shooting from west of the canyon had stopped. The men over there had pulled out to join the escaped pack train. He must have passed out. His whole side was numb now. Even the arm seemed dead. Then he grew aware of a crackling, steady run of sound, somewhere in the distance. It was shooting, and Durnbo had not had time to get back with help. As consciousness slipped away, Tracy wondered vaguely, drunkenly, if the outlaws had started fighting each other.

Chapter 19

A voice that seemed to be Ridge Durnbo's said gently, "Take it easy, pardner." Tracy opened his eyes to see firelight flicker on the familiar face, which was just above him. He groaned, and Durnbo said, "Easy, boy. All that's wrong's a busted leg, but you sure lost a few gallons of blood. That's what whipped you." The light kept dancing. Beyond it was darkness and, Tracy realized, a spread of stars. Somehow the day had gone, and night had come.

"Where — are we?" he managed to ask.

"Still at the lake," Durnbo said, "but with plenty of help, finally. You forget all that and rest."

"But how'd you — ?"

"I didn't." Durnbo laughed. "I'd hardly got to Lost River when the Baker Guards come bustin' along the trail. Give me a mount, and I come back with 'em. We caught that bunch of Rebs just outside the lavas. Guns and all, figurin' they had it cut. A few got away, but most're good Rebs now, dead, wounded or prisoners. We got the guns, to boot, which is more important. Looks like you about put down our rebellion all by yourself."

"Applegate's company," Tracy gasped. "How'd they know?"

Again came Durnbo's pleasing laugh. "I think that'll make good listenin' for you, what I've gathered. Tremaine's wife. She found out they had us out here and'd likely kill us. She went spankin' to Camp Baker and told 'em what was goin' on. Except for her, you wouldn't be here, old son. She's plenty all right."

"She — plenty more than — plenty. Tremaine — ?"

"He won't ever know she was more of a man than he was. He got here just ahead of us and found hisself fighting for his life, not for the glory of himself and Jeff Davis, in that order."

"He — ?"

"That's right. He's a good Reb, too." When Tracy started to ask more, Durnbo put his hand over his mouth, shaking his head. "That's enough. You nearly bled to death, *amigo.* You got to save your strength."

Tracy lay thinking of Lorna. He had known she had that kind of courage, and he had liked Durnbo's way of saying she stood tall above the ungrateful man to whom she had given so much. He pictured her while the drowsy vapors filled his mind, then everything slipped away again.

The next time Tracy was aware of anything but the pain that racked him, it was to realize that he was in bed. This time he opened his eyes against the full light of day. When he turned his head it was to discover that again there was someone near him. A woman. She sat at the head of the bed.

Feebly, he said, "Hello, Nan."

"Welcome home," Nan said.

"This your hotel?"

"No. We're in Doctor Willoughby's house in Jacksonville. You came in on a litter, this morning. It's now late afternoon. You were in a state of shock, the doctor says. If Ridge hadn't known where to look, you'd have laid up there on that lava and bled to death."

"There's a good man," Tracy mumbled.

"Yes. He says he had to save you. He wants you to come in with him and Jim in the cattle business."

"Love to, but — got a — war to fight, first."

Nan laughed. "What was that you just fought?"

"It must have been — a terrible experience — for Lorna."

The amusement left Nan's face. "It was, Tracy. But I think I helped her. Applegate made her stay at Camp Baker until the thing was settled. Naturally, they put her in the quarters they'd given me. She was so completely crushed that — well, I told her."

"About Tremaine and — you?"

Nan nodded. "She had to know he never loved anybody but himself. Not her, not me, although he betrayed her with me. And betrayed me by not telling me about her. She knew, then, that she hadn't been disloyal to anything that really existed. She felt a lot better."

"I'm glad. Nan, how about you?"

"I tried to give myself up to the sheriff. He wouldn't arrest me. He said I'd squared myself."

"I think so."

"I hope I have," she said humbly. Then she smiled and got to her feet. "Well, it's been a long time between meals for you. The doctor said to give you hot soup as soon as you woke up." She left him.

It was three weeks before Tracy was able to leave the doctor's house on crutches and move into a ground floor room at the Robinson House. After her bedside vigil during his crisis, Nan had gone back to Gold Hill. Ridge had driven her home in a buggy, and Tracy was glad that the pair had finally grown aware of each other. He had not seen Lorna, but he knew she had not left Jacksonville. He knew also that Tremaine's mines had been seized and his lieutenants arrested or scattered so widely they could never again make trouble.

It was yet another week before Tracy felt like going about the town, and one of his first calls was to Lorna's house. She was there, pale and drawn but recovering from a shock as deep as the one he had undergone. There wasn't much he could express of his deep and moving feelings except his gratitude for the act that had saved his life.

The only way he could do that was to say, "Thanks, Lorna," and let her guess what he meant. When she said nothing, he added, "I know it was a hard choice."

She looked at him quickly. "It was, but it shouldn't have been."

"You didn't know that till later."

"No. I suppose you'll be leaving."

"As soon as I'm fit for duty," he agreed. "But I've been afraid you'd leave before I saw you again and I'd lose track of you."

"No, I like the West. I'm staying here, although not in this house."

He smiled, his relief enormous. "Good. I'm coming back after the war, if my luck holds out. I'd like to go into the cattle business. Out there on the desert, where it was settled." They stood looking at each other. It was not a situation where they could say much more. But her face had eased. Her eyes again held life.

She said softly, "See you then, Tracy."

"Then, Lorna."

He turned and left the house.